ZOMG, IT ROX TO BE A GAMER GIRL!

Maddy's life: not so rockin'. Her parents split, she's stuck in a new, small town at a school full of Aberzombies and Haters, she has a crush on someone she really shouldn't like, and she's stuck with the nickname Freak Girl. Sometimes it's enough to retreat into her drawing—her manga is totally important to her—but when she gets Fields of Fantasy for her birthday, she knows she's found the one place she can be herself. In the game world, Maddy can transform from regular outcast high school student to Allora, a beautiful Elfin princess with magical powers to take down enemies with a snap of her fingers and a wave of her wand.

As Allora, Maddy's virtual life is perfect, and she even finds a little romance. But a real gamer girl understands that real life comes first—Maddy can't escape from her IRL problems. She has to find ways to kick back at the Haters, rock her manga, and find the new, real-life friends she knows she deserves.

GAMER GIRL

mari mancusi

• Dutton Children's Books •

DUTTON CHILDREN'S BOOKS
A division of Penguin Young Readers Group

Published by the Penguin Group
Penguin Group (USA) Inc., 375 Hudson Street, New York, New York 10014, U.S.A. |Penguin Group
(Canada), 90 Eglinton Avenue East, Suite 700, Toronto, Ontario, Canada M4P 2Y3 (a division of Pearson
Penguin Canada Inc.) | Penguin Books Ltd, 80 Strand, London WC2R 0RL, England | Penguin Ireland, 25
St Stephen's Green, Dublin 2, Ireland (a division of Penguin Books Ltd) | Penguin Group (Australia), 250
Camberwell Road, Camberwell, Victoria 3124, Australia (a division of Pearson Australia Group Pty Ltd)
Penguin Books India Pvt Ltd, 11 Community Centre, Panchsheel Park, New Delhi - 110 017, India | Penguin
Group (NZ), 67 Apollo Drive, Rosedale, North Shore 0632, New Zealand (a division of Pearson New
Zealand Ltd.) | Penguin Books (South Africa) (Pty) Ltd, 24 Sturdee Avenue, Rosebank, Johannesburg 2196,
South Africa | Penguin Books Ltd, Registered Offices: 80 Strand, London WC2R 0RL, England

This book is a work of fiction. Names, characters, places, and incidents are either the product of the author's
imagination or are used fictitiously, and any resemblance to actual persons, living or dead, business establishments,
events, or locales is entirely coincidental.

The publisher does not have any control over and does not assume any responsibility for author or third-
party websites or their content.

Library of Congress Cataloging-in-Publication Data

Mancusi, Marianne
Gamer girl / by Mari Mancusi.— 1st ed.   p. cm.
Summary: Struggling to fit in after her parents' divorce sends her from Boston to her grandmother's house in the
country, sixteen-year-old Maddy forms a manga club at school and falls in love through an online fantasy game.
ISBN 978-0-525-47995-6
Special Markets ISBN 978-0-525-42193-1
[1. Fantasy games—Fiction. 2. Role playing—Fiction. 3. Comic books, strips, etc.—Fiction.
4. High schools—Fiction. 5. Schools—Fiction. 6. Moving, Household—Fiction. 7. Divorce—Fiction.
8. Massachusetts—Fiction.] I. Title.
PZ7.M312178Gam 2008   [Fic]—dc22   2007050567

Published in the United States by Dutton Children's Books,
a division of Penguin Young Readers Group
345 Hudson Street, New York, New York 10014
www.penguin.com/youngreaders

Designed by Abby Kuperstock

Printed in USA

To all the irl gamer grrls out there who totally pwn the boyz. Hawt chix0rz FTW

GRANDMA'S HOUSE was a study of crystal and glass and contained 1,153 unicorns. I knew, because I counted one drizzly, dreary Thanksgiving when we were stuck inside waiting for the world's slowest turkey to brown. Horned beasts of crystal, glass, china, wood—she called them her "babies" and treasured them more than her dwindling life savings. (Dwindling mainly due to her unicorn habit. You wouldn't believe the prices of these things from the Franklin Mint.) Whenever we'd come over, she'd sit me down and show me her favorites.

She had a lot of favorites.

That was fine and tolerable when we lived an hour away and saw her once a year. Over the river and through the woods and all that. But now we were living with her. In her museumlike house. Surrounded by unicorns.

I suppose my story isn't unique. After all, half of marriages end in divorce, or so they say. Maybe I should count my blessings that Mom and Dad stuck it out as long as they did.

Still, having to vacate our über-hip Back Bay Boston brownstone, leave my private school and friends behind, and move to Unicorn Land—all in the middle of my sophomore year—was a bit much.

But I had no choice. Mom and Dad weren't speaking, unless they were yelling. Neither one could afford the mortgage on the brownstone, so they smacked down a For Sale sign and split—Dad to a smaller apartment down the street and Mom, me, and my eight-year-old sister, Emily, to New Hampshire. To Grandmother's house we go.

I can't even begin to tell you how painful that last day at my old school was. Saying good-bye to all my beloved teachers, promising my friends I'd IM and text at every possible second, cleaning out my locker, and tearing down the My Chemical Romance poster I'd stuck on the inside door on the first day of the school year. I'd been so full of hopes and dreams for the year back then. I was going to join the art club, write for the school paper, and, of course, make Ashley's older brother, David Silverman, my boyfriend. (Okay, the last one was a long shot, but you couldn't blame a girl for being goal oriented, could you?) It was going to be the best year ever.

Now, four months later, it was gearing up to be the worst.

"Maddy! You'd better get down here or you'll miss the bus!" Grandma called from downstairs, bringing me back to reality, aka my first day at Hannah Dustin High School. There were prisoners on death row more excited about their pending visit with the electric chair than I was about my enrollment.

I mean, hello! First off, there was a bus. An actual bus to take me from my middle-of-nowhere Grandma's house to my still-middle-of-nowhere school. Back home, I always walked. Met my friends at Dunkin' Donuts for French crullers and coffee, then giggled and gossiped all the way to the campus of Boston Academy. Now I'd actually have to board a smelly, fume-filled, environment-destroying bus to get to school. At least I was getting my license in a few weeks when I turned sixteen. Though my chances of getting Grandma to lend me the car were slim to none.

My cell buzzed, scattering all thoughts of transportation. I glanced down to see the text. From Caitlin.

GOOD LUCK ON FIRST DAY!

I smiled, feeling a tiny bit better. At least I had my friends. Sure, they were farther away from me now, but they still cared. I punched in Caitlin's number.

"Hey, girl," I said into the phone after she answered.

"Oh, hey, Mads, how's it going? How're the 'burbs? They arrest you for not wearing Gap yet? Turn your mom into a Stepford wife?" Caitlin had a habit of asking at least four questions in the same breath, making it impossible to answer any of them.

"Hardy-har-har," I replied. "You are too funny."

"What*evah*. At least I'm not funny-looking."

"Haven't looked in the mirror lately, have you?" I asked, with mock sympathy.

"I'm looking now, *bay-bee*. And I'm looking fine. DAMN fine."

I grinned, picturing my best friend dancing in front of the mirror as she was known to do, flaunting all that God had given her to anyone who cared to look. Caitlin was born without an insecurity gene. She died her hair pink and pierced her own nose in seventh grade. Her mother was totally cool with it, too, saying that girls needed to express themselves early in life so they could blossom into healthy, self-sufficient women who didn't need a man to complete them. (Caitlin's mother was also divorced—after her husband ran off to Vegas with his secretary. Some believed she was still a bit bitter about the whole thing.)

Hmm. Maybe my divorced mom would now let me explore the Manic Panic hair color rainbow, too. It'd be so cool to get some pink streaks in my hair. One time Caitlin and I went to Harvard Square after school and got the clip-on kind. Mom nearly had a heart attack until she found out they weren't real.

"Madeline!" Grandma again, this time sounding more insistent.

I groaned. "Sorry, Caits, gotta run before Grandma has kittens and starts sneezing to death."

"Okay, no prob," Caitlin said. "Good luck today. I hope you meet tons of über-cool rock girls and sexy, sexy bad boys."

"I'll settle for anyone not openly worshipping the gods of Aberzombie," I replied with a laugh. "I'll miss you guys. Don't have too much fun without me."

"Wouldn't dream of it. We'll mourn you all day and fast in your honor at lunchtime. Unless they're serving pizza, of course. If they're serving pizza, consider yourself gone and forgotten."

"Fair enough. I'll call you after school to let you know how it went."

"Cool. Later, gator."

I pressed End, grabbed my hoodie, and vacated the Pepto-Bismol-colored, unicorn-themed bedroom Grandma had stuck me in. Pretty nauseating, let me tell you, though I couldn't exactly complain. After all, originally she wanted me to share it with Emily. I think I would have stabbed myself with a unicorn horn if I had to bunk up with my little sis. Luckily for me, Emily wasn't so keen on the idea either and used her big mouth to voice her displeasure. Repeatedly. So Grandma cleaned out her sewing room and declared it Emily's. Kid had a gift for getting exactly what she wanted. I envied her that.

I started down the shag-carpeted stairs and found Grandma standing in the unicorn-infested living room below, a sentry guarding the path to freedom. And let's just say her stern, disapproving look could have been picked up by a satellite.

I glanced around for Mom, but she was nowhere to be found. Must have already left for work. Not good. I bit my lower lip, knowing exactly what was coming before the woman even opened her mouth.

"You're wearing *that* to school?"

"Uh . . . yes?" I really couldn't think of anything else to say. I prayed I was wrong about Mom being at work and that she'd suddenly come around the corner and assure Grandma that my look was perfectly acceptable for a twenty-first-century teen. But no luck.

Okay, fine, maybe I should have dressed a *tad* more conservative. We *were* in the suburbs after all. But image was everything in high school and I felt I needed to make the appropriate "This is who I am" statement from day one to attract the right friends. (Sad, but true.) So I'd donned a short plaid skirt, paired with Doc Marten boots and a zip-up hoodie over my Pooka the Goblin Cat baby doll tee. It said, *Gothy, but approachable.*

At least to me. Grandma was obviously getting a different message as she fanned herself with a wrinkly hand, shaking her head in disbelief. Eesh. You'd have thought I'd come downstairs in Britney Spears's last VMA outfit.

"Madeline Ann, you look like a dead prostitute," she declared.

I opened my mouth to defend and retort, but reluctantly closed it again. We'd been drilled by Mom since day one not to talk back to Grandma. *After all, she's sooo nice to let us live here. We need to respect her and her rules.*

"I don't know what kind of getup you wore back in that

city," Grandma said, spitting out the word *city* as if it were poison. "But you'll find kids in Farmingdale don't dress like that."

It was an effort not to roll my eyes. How did she know what kids wore? When was the last time she hung out at the local high school? I'd be willing to bet it was back when *Grease* was still the word. I looked longingly at the front door, wondering if I could just make a run for it. Grandma was old. Had arthritis. She probably couldn't catch me if I dashed outside and caught the bus just as it was picking up the neighbor kids down the street. . . .

Then, as if by a miracle, I heard a beep outside. Phew.

"The bus!" I cried. "Gotta go."

Grandma leaped in front of the door, effectively blocking my escape. For a lady approaching seventy, she sure could move quickly. "Not so fast," she said. "I'll drive you." She folded her arms across her chest. "After you change."

"But . . ."

"No buts. Now hop to it!"

My shoulders slumped. I wasn't going to win this, was I? I trudged over to the stairs, my feet feeling like they were made of lead. Out the window, I caught the bright yellow vision of freedom pulling away from the curb.

"You know," I remarked as I climbed, stair by stair, "I don't have anything in my closet you'd possibly approve of. Seriously. Most everything I own is black."

But Grandma had already thought of this. "Don't worry,

sweetie," she replied immediately. "You can borrow some of *my* clothes."

I stopped walking. Oh, no. No, no, no!

Sure enough, fifteen minutes later I'd been stuffed into a pair of bulky, pale blue "mom jeans" that came up past my belly button and a totally nonfitted oversized sweatshirt with—brace yourself here—frolicking unicorns embroidered on the front.

It couldn't get worse. It just couldn't.

I looked in the mirror, tears welling up in my eyes. "Please, Grandma. I can't wear this to school. Seriously."

"And why not?" she demanded, coming up behind me and straightening my sweatshirt. "I think you look adorable."

Of course you do. "Yeah, but they're . . ." I was about to say *old lady clothes*, but remembered Mom's warning not to offend. "No one my age would be caught dead in this kind of outfit," I amended. "If I show up like this, everyone's going to laugh at me."

"If they laugh at you, then they're not your friends." Grandma huffed. "Real friends don't judge people by what they wear, but what they're like on the inside."

There was a huge, gigantic flaw in that argument since *she* was the one who made me change clothes in the first place, but I realized it would do no good to point it out.

Instead, I looked back in the mirror, praying maybe I could pull it off as some kind of edgy street wear the kids in the 'burbs hadn't heard of yet. Like, *Dude, unicorns are so in right now, where have you been?* But it was no use. While I might have slid by with the unicorn thing, there was no way the mom jeans would escape notice.

I would have to kill myself on the way to school. Or run away and join the circus. Or . . .

A plan formed in my mind. As soon as Grandma dropped me off, I'd leave campus and find a store. There had to be stores around somewhere. Buy a decent outfit and head to class. I might have to miss first period, but it would be well worth it.

"Okay, let's go," Grandma said, jingling her keys.

Feeling better at having a plan, I joined her in her ancient Toyota and let her drive me to school. Ten minutes later she pulled into the parking lot. I looked up at the brick building on the hill. What would it be like? Would my teachers be cool? Would I find new friends? I looked down at my hands and realized they were shaking. I wished for the thousandth time I was wearing my normal clothes. I would have felt a hell of a lot more confident dressed as me.

I exited the car, thanking Grandma for the ride. To my dismay, she pulled the key out of the ignition and joined me on the curb.

"Um," I said, looking at her smiling face with concern. "What are you doing?"

"I thought I'd walk you into the office," she replied, obviously pleased with herself.

Oh, God. Oh, God. "You really don't have to—"

"I insist."

Of course she did. She also insisted on grabbing me by

the hand when we crossed the street and her iron grip didn't loosen as we approached the school. The sinking feeling in my stomach was getting worse.

I could feel the stares as soon as we reached the school entrance and heard the snickers. Not surprising, I guess. How often did you see a grandma dragging a unicorn-clad girl through the front doors of your local high school? They all probably thought I was special needs.

"We'll go to the principal's office and get your schedule," Grandma explained, as if I were a five-year-old on her first day of kindergarten. I hung my head and prayed for some kind of divine intervention. Maybe I was only dreaming. I'd wake up any second now, cozy in my bed, realizing this was all just one big, long, horrible nightmare.

But no such luck. I was really here. And the nightmare was my reality.

We stepped through the double doors, into a sea of lip-glossed Barbies and Tom Brady wannabes. I did a double take. Caitlin warned me this could happen, but I'd laughed her off. Surely every high school had some diversity, right?

Evidently wrong. It was as if I'd wandered into a living, breathing American Eagle commercial. Shudder. I looked around, desperately trying to pinpoint at least one person who would prefer Hot Topic over H&M, but came up empty.

Where were the mop-headed emo boys and Edward Cullen-worshipping Goth girls? Where were the skater kids? The punk rockers?

I felt a lump rise to my throat. This was so not good.

Anger burned in my gut. Stupid Mom for leaving Dad. Maybe if Mom wasn't in such a hurry to skip town, they could have gotten counseling or something. Worked it out. Then I'd be back in Boston right now, in my old school, laughing with my old friends, without a care in the world.

Instead of rotting away in my current hell.

The sea of kids parted, suddenly, almost diving out of the way. I look down the newly formed path, raising my eyebrows. Four kids—two boys and two girls—sauntered down the hallway in a way you usually only see in teen movies. Heads high, shoulders back, self-satisfied smirks written across their perfect faces. They might as well have been wearing T-shirts with the word *popular* scrawled across the front.

"Who are they?" I wondered aloud, forgetting Grandma for a moment.

"You must be new," a Buddy Holly/Elvis Costello lookalike to my right chuckled. The only kid I'd seen so far that even remotely stood out from the rest of the clones. "That's Hannah Dustin High's royal court. Billy, Chad, Lucy, and Chelsea. In that order. They pretty much rule the school."

That much was obvious, given the awed stares of the rest of the kids. I studied the four of them closer. Lucy wore a cheerleading outfit. No shock there. Chelsea, on the other hand, was channeling her inner Jackie O, dressed to impress with a pristine pink suit, complete with a requisite string of pearls and a dainty white clutch in her well-manicured hand. It should have looked old-fashioned, but the girl totally worked it.

I turned my attention to the two boys. Billy was tanned, tall and muscular, good-looking—your typical jock meathead, really—wearing a Patriots jersey and camouflage pants. And Chad . . .

My breath hitched as my eyes fell on Chad. He was tall, too, but lean—like a cat, almost—carrying himself with the slinky grace of a model or movie star. He had curly blond hair and piercing blue eyes, framed with long sooty lashes. A chiseled face with perfectly sculpted cheekbones and a full mouth that looked perfectly kissable.

I shivered. Utterly delicious.

Not that it mattered. I mean, let's face it. Even if I *were* dressed in my normal clothes and not unicorn chic, no one like him would ever go out with someone like me. I was a skater kid's girlfriend, not the homecoming queen. And this wasn't some bad eighties Molly Ringwald movie like *Pretty in Pink*.

Besides, I reminded myself as I forced my gaze away from his beautiful face, he was probably dumb and spoiled and used to girls fawning over him. Good-looking guys usually were. Especially if they found themselves in the popular clique, as this guy had. I'm sure he would annoy the hell out of me the second he opened his mouth.

Still, I had to admit, there was just something about him. . . .

I realized the four of them had stopped in front of me. Oh, joy. Time to be sized up and judged by the popular clique.

This day was getting more and more like a bad after-school special every minute. After the commercial break, I'd probably start drinking and doing drugs, just to fit in, only to have my best friend die and my mother convince me to head to rehab and restart my life, friendless, sober, and alone, but strangely happy and peaceful about it all.

"Nice shirt." Chelsea sniffed, giving me a once-over.

"Yeah, I think my five-year-old sister has one just like it," Lucy added snottily.

"Hey, leave the girl alone," Billy said with a smirk. "It's obvious she's corny!" He cracked up at his own lame joke. "Get it? Corny? Like the unicorn on her shirt?" He high-fived Chad, who seemed a bit reluctant to slap his hand back. Or maybe it was just my imagination.

In the meantime, the hallway erupted in laughter and jeers, totally egging him on. I could feel my face burning with humiliation as I stared at my feet, wishing to be anywhere in the world but here. I couldn't believe it. Two minutes into my new school year and I was already the class joke.

I suddenly realized Grandma was squinting at Billy intently. At first I thought she might be considering coming to my aid. But then her face lit up and she squealed, "Billy? Billy Henderson? Is that you?" to my new arch nemesis.

I cringed. I had no idea what was coming, but I knew it couldn't be good.

Sure enough, Billy stiffened. "Hi, Mrs. Miller," he mumbled out of the corner of his mouth. I cocked my head in question. The two of them knew each other? A split second later, Grandma had let go of my hand to crush Billy into a tight embrace. Guess so.

"Oh, Billy," she crowed, releasing him from the hug. "It's so good to see you! You're all grown up now. Last time I saw you, you were four feet tall and still wetting the bed!"

Laughter broke out among the crowd and Billy's face darkened to a beet red. I gaped in horror. This was not happening. This could not be happening. My grandma, embarrassing the most popular kid in school. On my first day.

Billy whirled around to face the crowd. "Shut up!" he growled. "She's lying. I swear."

Was it too late to pretend the old woman had Alzheimer's and had just wandered into school by mistake? Absolutely no relation to me whatsoever?

"Billy, this is my granddaughter Maddy."

Evidently it was.

She shoved me forward, having no idea about the scene she was causing. "Maddy, do you remember Billy from back when you were little? He used to live down the street. I babysat him while his mother was at work."

I stared at Billy. He stared back at me, his face a mixture of humiliation and fury. I read his expression clear as day. I was the one who would pay for this public embarrassment. And I would pay dearly. After all, the others might have eventually forgotten my fashion faux pas, but Billy would never forget this.

"Come on, Grandma," I said, steering her toward the door marked MAIN OFFICE. "I need to get my schedule."

"Come on, Grandma," Billy mocked in a high-pitched voice as the elderly woman turned away. "Let's go home and play with unicorns."

I glared at him, wanting nothing more than to smack him upside the head and wipe that ugly smirk off his face. But what good would it do, really? There was no winning for me in this situation and I knew it. So I sucked up my pride and turned away, following Grandma into the office, where she was talking to a secretary. "I think you're all set now, Madeline," she declared, handing me a slip of paper. "I've done my grandmotherly duties. Now you behave yourself on your first day."

I sighed and took the schedule. "Thanks, Grandma," I said.

"Have a great day, sweetie, and I'll see you back at the house tonight." Stepping out into the hall, she called out, "I'll even make you your favorite bunny rabbit cookies."

Ah, yes, the bunny rabbit cookies I liked back when I was six years old. The icing on the anticool cake.

"Bye, Grandma," I said, resigning myself to my fate of school loser.

I reluctantly stepped into the hallway and faced the masses again.

"Aren't you going to say good-bye to Grandma?" Chelsea was teasing Billy, nudging him in the ribs. He glowered at her.

"Shut up," he growled. "I don't even know who that crazy loon was."

"She certainly seemed to know you."

"Billy wets the bed, Billy wets the bed," Lucy chimed in, in a singsong voice.

"SHUT UP!" Billy roared. He met my eyes with his, furious and full of hatred. "You are so dead, Freak Girl," he muttered under his breath. Then he pushed by me and into the crowd, which parted for him as it did before. His gang followed him, still giggling. Chad lagged behind, glancing backward. He caught my eye, gave a sheepish shrug, and mouthed the word "Sorry." Then he and his friends turned the corner and disappeared.

I stared after them, shocked by Chad's apology. I had so not expected that. Maybe he was different from his friends. Not that it mattered. Nice or not, he was way out of my league and I knew it.

Still, he was so cute. So, so cute.

"Wow, way to make a first impression," said a voice to my right as the crowd dispersed. I looked over to see the Elvis Costello boy on my right. He wore a black turtleneck, dark blue jeans, and thick black glasses over his brown eyes. Very hipster-nerd chic. "I'm Matt," he said, holding out a hand. "And you, Maddy, have just embarrassed the most powerful kid in school."

"I didn't say anything," I protested weakly, knowing that it didn't matter. I was guilty by association, and while Billy couldn't retaliate against Grandma, he could and would make my life horrible. I just knew it. "This is so not how I wanted my first day to begin."

"Meh, it's really not about you, you know. Those guys hate pretty much everyone not in their immediate social circle. And that means ninety-five percent of the school. Funny, when you consider the same ninety-five percent loves them and worships the ground they walk on."

I made a face. "Well, not me. Count me in for hating the haters, thank you very much." Except maybe Chad. He was different. But I wasn't about to admit that to Matt.

"The Haters." Matt chuckled. "That's a fitting name actually." The bell rang, cutting him off. "Gotta get to class," he said, winking at me. "See you around. And don't let the Haters get you down."

I'D LOVE to say my day got better from there, but it would be a lie. I felt like a leper as I walked through the halls. I could feel people pointing and whispering as I passed. And why wouldn't they? I was wearing a silly unicorn sweatshirt. And I'm sure there wasn't a soul in school who hadn't now heard of Grandma's taking on Billy Henderson.

I tried using my cell phone to call Caitlin—to at least get a comforting ear—only to have it confiscated by a teacher who told me that here at Hannah Dustin, cell phones needed to be kept in lockers until the end of the day. I tried sneaking out of school to buy a new outfit, only to be stopped and told there was no open campus here. I was trapped. A POW with unicorns on my chest. It probably could have been worse, but I wasn't sure how.

After what seemed an eternity, the final bell rang. I retrieved my cell phone from the office, then caught the early bus home. Mom greeted me at the door.

"How was your first day?" she asked, her cheerful expression not completely masking her tired eyes. Then she looked down at the frolicking unicorns on my chest. "That's a new look for you." She smirked.

I opened my mouth to tell her about how awful it had been, then I saw Grandma lurking in the hallway behind her. "Fine," I muttered instead. "I've got homework." I pushed past her and headed up to my room.

"Fine?" Mom called after me. "That's all? What did you think of your teachers? Were the kids nice? Did you make any new friends?"

Anger burned in my gut at her questions. I knew she had no idea, but I couldn't help blaming her for asking. After all, she was the one who forced me to attend this miserable school to begin with. To leave my friends behind.

"Oh, sure," I said, my voice dripping with sarcasm. "Tons of friends. In fact, I'm a shoo-in for homecoming."

"Maddy, come back here and talk to me!" Mom called after me.

I ignored her, taking the steps two at a time until I reached the top landing and ran to my room. I flopped on my bed and grabbed my cell out of my purse and dialed Caitlin.

"Hello?" my friend answered a moment later, sounding out of breath and giggly.

"Hey, Cait," I said.

"Mads!" she cried. "How's it going? Oh, wait—hang on. . . ." I could hear her talking in the background. "Okay, sorry," she said. "How did your first day go?"

"Dude, it was horrible!" I moaned. "First, Grandma

made me wear this shirt that had unicorns on it, and then—"

"Sorry, Mads, hang on one more time." More muffled conversation and giggles. Then she came back on the line. "Sorry. Me and Ashley are at J.P. Licks and we're trying to figure out ice-cream flavors."

A pang of loneliness shot through me. I should have been there with them. Eating ice cream and giggling. Probably flirting with Jon, that guy behind the counter we all had crushes on. But no! I was stuck in the middle of nowhere in a house that was more like a museum, after the worst day of school in my entire life.

"It's okay," I replied. A total lie. "I'll wait."

"Actually, can I just call you back later?" Caitlin asked. "Like, tonight or something? Or, um, tomorrow morning?"

"Sure," I said glumly.

"Cool. Later, gator." And with that, the phone disconnected, before I even had a chance to say good-bye. And somehow I knew in my heart she'd forget to call me back later. I was out of Boston. Out of their lives. Forgotten already.

I was totally and utterly alone.

A knock sounded on my door. I tried to ignore it, but Mom was never much for respecting space. She barged in and sat down on the side of my bed, studying me with pitying eyes. I rolled over to face the wall so she couldn't see I'd been crying.

"Bad first day?" she asked, sympathetically.

"Why do you care?"

"Maddy, of course I care. Don't be like that."

"If you cared, you wouldn't have dragged us here to the middle of nowhere and let Grandma humiliate me." I quickly related what had transpired.

Mom let out a sigh. "I'm sorry about that, Maddy," she said, reaching over to touch me on the shoulder. I jerked away. "I didn't realize she'd take it upon herself to dress you and bring you to school. But she does mean well."

"Um, great. That makes me feel so much better."

"She's old and she doesn't understand. But she has a good heart."

I rolled over to face her. "Mom, she embarrassed me in front of the whole school and I wore embroidered unicorns all day!"

Mom sighed again. "I'll have a talk with her," she said. "It won't happen again, I promise."

"Don't you see? It's too late! The damage is done."

"Don't overreact. I'm sure it couldn't have been that bad."

"You weren't there. You don't know."

"What do you want me to do, Maddy?" Mom asked, defensiveness creeping into her voice.

That was easy. "Don't make me go back there. Let me go to my old school."

Mom shook her head. "That's not possible."

Please. It wasn't possible only because she was too selfish. Because she decided to take off on my dad and refuse to try to work things out. And we all had to suffer for it.

"I'll wake up early and take the commuter train in," I suggested. "I don't mind."

"It's not the commute. Your old school costs a lot of money. I can't afford the tuition."

I gave up. "Fine. Whatever," I growled.

"Maddy . . ."

"I'm tired. I want to take a nap." I turned back on my side. I knew I was being childish, but at the moment, I didn't care. "Go ruin someone else's life for a while."

Mom sat there, unmoving. I could feel her stare at my back. Then she slowly got up and left the room.

Once she was gone, I rose from my bed and pulled my sketchbook out of my bag. I sat down at my desk and started drawing. It was the only thing, sometimes, that could pull me out of a bad mood. When I picked up a pen, it was like I entered an alternate universe. All of life's problems faded to the background and I lost myself in my art.

I was especially fond of Japanese-style art and had been creating my own manga. A graphic novel, if you will. I'd been writing a fantastical story about a girl who gets sucked into an alternate reality and has to fight demons and monsters. But today I found it hard to work on. Maybe because my own demons kept coming to the surface. And so I turned the page and started sketching a scene from school. Walking into school with Grandma, wearing the unicorn shirt. Billy mouthing off, me looking mortified.

I sighed, staring down at the drawing. I really should have done something. Told him off. Threatened violence. Showed him he couldn't intimidate me. But no, I was a coward. A stupid coward.

Inspired, I ripped off a new sheet of paper and sketched how the scene should have gone. This time, instead of me slumping my shoulders and playing the coward, I stood up to Billy. Pushed him back. Told him to leave me alone. I drew in the other kids' faces. Impressed. Awed. They'd never seen anyone stand up to Billy before. I was their hero.

I laughed as I looked down at my drawing. It was silly, for sure. But in a weird way it made me feel a tiny bit better.

THIS ONE'S from your father."

My mother shoved the brightly colored box at me as if it were a hot potato she was anxious to be rid of. Not surprising, I guess. Since their divorce, she treated most of Dad's stuff in this manner. You should have seen the yard sale she held the day after he moved out. The shoppers were shocked to be handed expensive parting gifts as they left the brownstone—"just for stopping by." Dad was pretty surprised, when he came back to collect his stuff and found out it'd all been sold or given away to people who Mom said obviously needed it more.

I accepted the gift from her, shaking it gently as I sat back down on Grandma's shag-carpeted living room floor, anxious to figure out what was inside the haphazardly taped-together box. Despite being born gift-wrap challenged, Dad always came through with the best presents ever. And he never cheated either, asking what I wanted before heading to the store like some clueless grown-ups did. He just instinctively seemed to know exactly what I'd want before I knew that "what" even existed.

"Open it!" urged my younger sister, Emily, from her crossed-legged position next to Grandma on the couch. At age eight, she had naturally curly, white-blond hair and naturally zero patience for anything that didn't directly involve her. In fact, I was pretty surprised she'd made it this long through the gift-opening portion of my sixteenth birthday celebration. No doubt Mom had bribed her with promises of ice cream and chocolate cake for when we were through. For ice cream and chocolate cake, Emily would have sat through a reading of the Constitution. Backward and with debates on each amendment in between.

"Come *on!*" Emily shouted, sounding more annoyed this time. "And don't do that thing where you slowly tear off each piece of tape to save the wrapping paper."

"Now, Emily. There's nothing wrong with recycling the paper," Grandma scolded her. "Wrapping paper doesn't just grow on trees, you know."

Actually I was pretty sure it did—at least indirectly— but there was no need to get into that kind of debate with Grandma. Mom would only get annoyed and then we'd have to have that talk again about how lucky we were to have Grandma to stay with after we had to sell the house because of the divorce. Oh, yes, so very lucky.

To satisfy Emily, I made a great show of tearing through the paper, crumpling it into a ball, and throwing it at her. After dodging her return throw, I looked down at my present. I squinted at the box for a moment and then broke out into a wide smile when I recognized what it was. "Fields of Fantasy!" I said, reading the name emblazoned on the box. "All right!"

My mom groaned. "A video game? He sent you a video game? After I told him time and time again that you needed socks and underwear?"

"I have *plenty* of underwear, Mom," I muttered, turning over the box to read the back. Not to mention that even if I were down to my last pair, I had zero desire for my father to be the one wandering through Vicky Secrets, selecting new ones. I mean, what if he got me, like, a thong or something? I would literally be required to die of embarrassment right then and there and that would be the end of it.

"But still! A video game?" Mom scowled. "Well, that just goes to show you, your father *has* never and *will* never grow up. He's always messing around with those computer games. Now he's recruiting you, I guess."

It was about time, too, I thought but didn't say. I'd begged Dad to let me play Fields of Fantasy since he got the game himself a year ago. But he kept insisting I wasn't old enough to join an online gaming community like this. Too many foul-mouthed, inappropriate adult players, he said, and wouldn't relent, even after I informed him I'd already heard every swear under the sun in high school. Finally, he promised, after weeks of my whining, that once I turned sixteen he'd let me play. But I figured he'd long forgotten and had no idea he'd buy me my own copy. What a great birthday present.

I noticed a card had fallen from the gift. I tore it open and read Dad's note.

Dear Maddy,

Okay, kiddo! I promised you the game and here it is! Once you create a character we can play together. This way, even though we don't live in the same house anymore, we can still hang out virtually whenever we want!!!

So go ahead—what are you waiting for?

Install the game on your computer and meet me in the FIELDS OF FANTASY!

Love,

Dad (aka RockStarBob)

"Wow, that's so cool," I remarked, trying to peel off the sticky tape holding the box closed. "I need to check this out now." Yup, once again Dad managed to come through with the most original, most rocking present. And what a great idea—to find a way to meet up online. He must have missed me as much as I missed him.

"You have ten minutes," Mom told me. "Then it's time for cake." She rose from her seat, signaling that the present-opening portion of our evening had ended. Guess she really *wasn't* trying to trick me when she swore up and down that she hadn't bought me an iPod for my birthday or signed me up for driver's ed. Doomed to exist another year being the only sophomore alive who was still sporting a practically antique Discman. And there sure wasn't a new car in the driveway either.

Don't get me wrong. I wasn't one of those spoiled *My Super Sweet 16* kids you saw on MTV. I knew money was tight and the last thing I wanted to do was make Mom feel bad for not being able to provide for us. The woman worked two jobs, just to keep us in clothes and shoes. But at the same time I couldn't help but be a little resentful. After all, if she hadn't ditched Dad, there'd be plenty of money for high-end electronics. Not to mention a house we didn't have to share with Grandma. Back in my hometown. With my friends.

Actually, make that my former friends. As in the ones who didn't even bother to show up for my birthday party. I'd IMed both Caitlin and Ashley a week ago to invite them and they swore they'd be here. But then about a half hour before the party, they both texted me—Caitlin couldn't get a ride. Ashley was "sick."

Yeah, right. How convenient. Especially when I went on Facebook and saw there was a big party at David Silverman's house tonight. Traitors. But, hey, I probably would have ditched my own party for that, so I couldn't really blame them. I just wished they'd had the guts to tell me the truth.

I sighed and scrambled to my feet, stepping over piles of discarded wrapping paper, pink sweaters from Old Navy that I'd never wear, the Barbie from Grandma, who failed to realize that I was no longer eight, and the designer clothes for Barbie from Emily, who *was* eight and obviously plotted to steal both doll and wardrobe as soon as my back was turned and thus make even *my* birthday all about her.

After throwing out a generic thank-you, I headed upstairs to my bedroom and switched on my computer, slipped the game disc into the CD drive, and started the install. The computer was a divorce gift from Dad, though Mom preferred to refer to it as a bribe, saying it was way too high end to simply do homework on. I was glad to have it now, though. Fields of Fantasy had some demanding system requirements.

As I waited for the disc to install, I skimmed through the instructions. It was an adventure game, a sort of Dungeons & Dragons meets *Lord of the Rings* type thing. You played online, creating a character to fight monsters and win treasure. I'd watched Dad play for hours—he was totally addicted—and it always looked like such fun. I was thrilled to finally have a chance to become a gamer girl myself. Not to mention it would be great to get some quality alone time with Dad—something that rarely happened even during our weekend visits, mostly because Emily was endlessly demanding something to steal Dad's attention away from me.

My computer chirped at me, confirming the game had been loaded and was ready to play. I clicked on the desktop icon and logged on.

The program launched and stopped at a player selection screen, prompting me to design my new character. There were lots of different-looking types to choose from. Some were human, while others were random species—elves, halflings, orcs, even undead creatures.

I decided to go with a female elf, giving her long blond hair and sparkling blue eyes. She had a pouty red mouth, big breasts, and a skinny waist. About as different as you could get from black-haired, brown-eyed, flat-chested, real-life me. Which was exactly what I was looking for, actually. This way I could prance around the virtual world with ease, masked as an ethereal goddess. And no one online would have any clue what an ugly duckling hid behind the flawless elfin face.

Now if only I could send my character to school. All the boys would go wild over me. That would sure show the Haters (as I now liked to call them).

No, school had not gotten any better, in case you were wondering. My third week into Hannah Dustin was just as bad as my first. I had yet to make a single friend and each and every day the Haters would go out of their way to torture me. My only consolation was all the inspiration it was giving me for my art—which had become full of the best comebacks and revenges on Billy. On paper, I was the most popular girl in school.

I turned back to the game, not wanting to think about school. It was time to give my alter-ego elf goddess a job. I studied the choices presented. She could be a brave, fearless knight, a holy, healing priest, or a wise and all-powerful magician. I glanced at the elf. She was so skinny, I wasn't sure about her wielding some huge sword. And she was certainly way too sexy to be a priest. That left magician.

Having made all of my selections, I had to pick a name. I wanted something cooler than simply Maddy—which always sounded more like an anger management problem than a name to me. Finally, after some thought, I chose Allora—which was beautiful and exotic and fit my elf perfectly.

After a dramatic introduction with sword clashing and spell casting and rather thrilling music, the game cut to a cartoon scene of Allora, standing in a small, colorful elfin village. She was dressed in a low-cut red robe and carrying a big stick. She looked up at me and smiled, giving me a sly wink, as if she knew I was there, watching, ready to take control of her destiny. Kind of weird, actually. But at the same time pretty cool.

I used the mouse and keyboard, as the instructions stated, to run Allora around the village. There were thatch-roofed huts, grassy paths, and droopy weeping willow trees with cartoon faces carved into their trunks. I bumped into several other characters, dressed in medieval-style gear, also wandering about. A man in a beige tunic winked at me. A woman in chain mail waved hello. I stopped, realizing that all of the characters on-screen were being controlled by real-life people, logged on from their own computers in their own homes. I watched in amazement for a moment as the various elves, halflings, and humans bustled about town, going about their business as if this were their everyday existence.

Who were these people? Where did they come from? And what possessed them to take on a character and play this game? Were they bored? Lonely? Did they seek adventure? New friends? Or were they just trying to escape real life for a few hours?

The whole concept was so cool. Being part of an online community where people mingled and made friends with those they'd never met in real life. In the game, no one had any clue who I was, and they didn't care either. I wasn't a loser who hadn't made a single friend at her new school. I was a beautiful elfin princess who was studying to be a mage. And no one had any idea I once spent a whole day wearing frolicking unicorns on my chest.

I smiled. So cool. I couldn't wait to thank Dad for getting me the game. In fact, maybe he was online right now. I scanned his letter to find his character's name.

RockStarBob.

Oh-kay then. Not the name I would have picked for a medieval fantasy character, but whatever. I followed the instructions and typed him a message using the game's instant messaging feature.

[Allora] Hey, Dad! I got the game!

[RockStarBob] Hey, kiddo! I'm glad! How do you like it so far?

[Allora] Well, I just logged on, so I haven't really done much exploring.

[RockStarBob] Ah.

[Allora] Um, do you want to come . . . meet me . . . I guess?

[RockStarBob] Um . . .

[RockStarBob] Hang on a sec, hon.

[RockStarBob] kk, back. Um, I didn't realize you'd be online now. So I started playing with some friends. We're in this big dungeon, right in the middle of fighting some monsters.

[Allora] Oh. Okay. Can I come watch you?

[RockStarBob] Heh. No, sweetie. You're too low a level. You'd never make it in alive.

[Allora] Oh.

[RockStarBob] Um, why don't you play by yourself for a bit and level up? And then later in the week we can play together. I can meet you after school on Thursday, around five. Just go to the Elf Tree Café, okay? I'll meet you there.

[Allora] Okay! Cool. Sounds good. See you then! Thanks for the game!

[RockStarBob] You're welcome, kiddo. I think you're going to love it!

"Maddy! Cake time!" my mother called. Reluctantly, I logged off the game and trudged downstairs. I guess it was too much to expect my dad would just be sitting around waiting for me to log on. After all, how would he know when we were celebrating my birthday? Not like Mom sent him an Evite. And he did say he'd meet me Thursday. That'd be cool.

At the very least, it would give me something to look forward to when trying to survive yet another week of high school.

In what state of mind is Romeo when we first meet him?"

Monday morning and I was in English class, sketching in the margins of my notepad while our teacher drilled us on the finer points of Shakespeare's *Romeo and Juliet*.

"Anyone?" Ms. Reilly asked, looking over the rows of bored students. She ran a hand through her curly red hair. She was really young for a teacher and I guessed still under the naive impression that she could actually make a difference in her students' lives. Of course soon enough she'd realize her role here was little more than glorified babysitter and she'd start practicing the method the old-school teachers favored, like wheeling in a television and letting us watch the movie version of whatever was on the curriculum that week.

"Come on, did anyone do this weekend's reading assignment?"

I did, nerd that I am. Not that I'd needed to. I'd read the play four times over the last three years and had seen both the 1968 movie and the way-cool Leonardo DiCaprio/Claire Danes modern update. There was just something about the tragic love story that really spoke to me.

But that didn't mean I was going to raise my hand and call attention to myself. I had enough notoriety at Hannah Dustin High already, thank you very much.

A crumpled piece of paper bounced onto my desk. I didn't have to turn around to know Billy and his cronies were responsible. Ever since that first day in school, when Grandma had told all his friends about his bed-wetting problem, he'd made it his life's mission to annoy and embarrass me. And he and his Hater friends were good at the job. I'd had my lunch tray tipped over four times, countless spitballs in my hair, my locker Super Glued shut, and my clothes stolen from my gym locker and stuffed down the toilet. All in the span of three weeks.

While I had never been the most popular girl back in my old school, at least I had my circle of friends. Girls to giggle with in the hallways and boys to pass notes to in class. Now I had no one. Not even my old friends, who were too wrapped up in their own daily lives to ever remember to call me back. And when they eventually did, they had new stories and new inside jokes—ones I didn't know or understand. I'd hang up the phone after talking to them, feeling even more alone than before.

Against my better judgment, I unfolded the paper. Someone had drawn a picture of a vampire girl that was obviously supposed to be me. The words FREAK GIRL were printed in big block letters across the page. *Jerks.* I crumpled up the paper in my fist, my face burning. Laughter erupted from the back of the classroom. I forced myself not to turn around.

"And what, pray tell, is so funny, William?" demanded Ms. Reilly, suddenly stopping her lesson. She made her way through the rows of desks until she reached my nemesis and his gang. I stole a glance. All the boys had immediately donned poker faces. Innocent angels, the lot of them.

"Nothing, Ms. Reilly," they chimed.

She turned back to me. "Were these boys bothering you, Maddy?" she queried. I squirmed in my seat. Oh, great. This was the last thing I needed. Teacher intervention.

"No, Ms. Reilly," I said, silently begging her to go back to her lesson. *Don't make it worse,* I prayed. *Please don't make it worse.*

She narrowed her eyes. Of course she didn't believe me. She held out her hand and I reluctantly handed over the vampire drawing. After a brief inspection, she turned back and looked straight at Billy. "Wow, someone's quite the artist," she remarked pointedly. "Would you like to tell me who drew this?"

Billy's friends started laughing. Billy hissed at them to shut up. Ms. Reilly turned back to me. "Madeline," she said, "did William throw this at you?"

I grimaced, realizing my predicament. I didn't want to lie—especially not to Ms. Reilly, who was cool and interesting and tried hard to be a good teacher. But on the other hand, I wasn't a snitch. And the last thing I wanted was to piss off Billy even more. It would only end badly for me.

I made my decision. "No, I don't know who drew it," I said, sinking lower into my seat and praying she'd take my answer without pressing me further.

Ms. Reilly looked down at me for a moment, silent pity clear in her eyes. Great. She felt bad for me. Could I get any more pathetic?

"I know who drew it."

Heads turned to the opposite side of the room. Matt, the hipster kid I met my first day here, was madly waving his hand in the air, ignoring Billy's death look.

"It was Billy Henderson," he announced, triumph clear in his voice. I smiled a little. He was the only person I'd seen so far who dared stand up to the Haters. Probably because he was the only person who didn't buy into their whole high school royalty thing to begin with. I decided to make an effort to talk to him later. After all, he definitely had good-friend potential.

"Shut up, dork," Billy retorted, glowering at the tattle-taler.

Ms. Reilly's head pivoted sharply. "William," she scolded. "What did I tell you about name calling?"

Billy opened his mouth to retort, but evidently thought better of it. "Sorry," he muttered. I noticed Matt giving him a friendly wave from behind Ms. Reilly's back, and stifled a giggle.

"Billy, I want you to go down to the principal's office and explain your need to express yourself artistically in class," the teacher ordered. "Perhaps we could sign you up for after-school art classes or something."

Now the whole class was laughing. Billy scowled at the teacher, but didn't object.

The bell rang then and everyone jumped up, eager to leave so they could go out in the halls and gossip about the whole thing to their friends. I gathered my books as quickly as possible, trying to get out of there before Billy came down the aisle. Also, I wanted to find Matt and thank him for coming to my rescue.

"Madeline, could I talk to you for a moment before you leave?" Ms. Reilly asked. My shoulders slumped. So much for that plan.

"Yeah, sure," I said, seeing no other option.

Billy pushed by me to exit, deliberately knocking my *Romeo and Juliet* book from my hands. It fell to the floor and he stamped on it with a dirty boot, ripping the cover. "Oh, I'm so sorry," he said loudly. Under his breath he added, "You're so dead, Freak Girl."

I sighed. I should have known, even though I'd kept my mouth shut and it was Matt who saw fit to sell him out, that Billy was still going to blame me.

I reached down and picked my book up off the floor. Ms. Reilly walked over to me and sat down at the desk beside me.

"I've, um, really got to get to my next class . . ." I tried.

"I'll write you a pass."

Sigh. "Okay." I sank back into my chair.

Ms. Reilly smoothed out Billy's drawing on the desk, shaking her head. "He's not a very good artist, is he?" she remarked. "In fact, I think I've seen kindergarten finger painters with more talent."

I chuckled, despite myself, and took the drawing from her. It really was pretty hideous. "Yeah, he has zero sense of composition," I analyzed. "And his lines are all shaky."

Ms. Reilly looked pointedly at me. "You, on the other hand, I hear, are really good. Mr. Thomas was telling me about the manga sketches you did for him the other day."

I felt my face heat. The art teacher talked about me to the other teachers? "I'm okay, I guess," I replied, recrumpling Billy's stupid drawing. "I mean, it's something I like doing."

"Well, I'd love to see some of your stuff sometime," Ms. Reilly said. "If you don't mind showing me. I really love manga."

I was surprised. Most adults didn't even know what manga was, and if they did, they dismissed it as comic book trash. "Sure, I mean, I guess." I never had anyone to show my drawings to. My friends back in Boston didn't really care and my parents only oohed and ahhed because that's what parents were supposed to do when a child makes an effort to express herself. But Ms. Reilly seemed genuinely interested. Kind of cool.

The teacher leaned forward. "Maddy, I know high school can be a tough time. Especially when you're new. Believe me, I know."

Aha! I knew this conversation wasn't really about art. "I'm fine," I replied automatically. I so did not want to get into it all with her, no matter how much she appreciated manga.

She sighed. "You're very bright. And creative. And sweet." She reached over and patted me on the arm. "Look, I'm here for you if you want to talk. About anything. And whatever you say to me stays here. In the vault. I won't tell your parents or the principal. I just . . . well, I'm here if you need a friend."

I knew she was trying to help. That she was sincere. But it was just too hard. I mean, what was I supposed to say? Tell her how everyone thought I was a freak and that I had no friends? Yeah, right. I felt tears well up in my eyes and swiped them away.

"Thanks. I . . . I mean, that's nice of you. But I'm fine. Really." I shifted in my seat, swallowing back the lump in my throat. "Can I go now?"

She studied me for a moment, her face sad. Why did she care so much? "Yes, you can go now," she said at last. "But my offer remains open, okay? And don't forget—I want to see your art sometime soon."

"Okay." I jumped up from the seat and made a dash for the exit. It was nice of her to offer to talk. But at the end of the day, she was a grown-up. A teacher. She would never understand.

No one would.

5

HEY, FREAK Girl, whatcha doing?"

Lunchtime on Thursday, later that week. I looked up to see Billy and the Haters approach the cafeteria table. I'd deliberately chosen a seat in the very back, away from their crowd, so I could lay low and work on my manga. I was drawing a portrait of Allora, my Gamer Girl. But a seat on Mars wouldn't have been far enough away for Billy. Especially not after Monday's incident in English class.

"Yeah, Freak Girl. Why are you back here by yourself? No friends?" Flanking Billy were the rest of the Haters, of course. Rarely did you see one stray far from the pack. They even took a lot of the same classes. Lucy was dressed in her requisite cheerleading captain's outfit. (I swear she wore it even when they didn't have practice, just for status.) Chelsea had on some kind of filmy pink baby doll dress that probably cost more than my entire wardrobe put together. She came from old money, I'd learned, and liked to tell people that her ancestors came over on the *Mayflower*, as if that were some big accomplishment that automatically made her cool. Because, like, Pilgrim chicks were so the It girls of their time.

And then there was Chad.

Yes, yes, I was still sporting that pathetic, hopeless crush on the kid. I knew it was wrong. He was way out of my league and not even really my type. Caitlin would have had a field day if she knew—telling me to go for a skater or something and leave the Aberzombie to the cheerleaders. But I couldn't help it. I couldn't shake the butterflies that danced a disco beat in my stomach every time he came near. Pathetic, but true.

"Hey, Corny, I'm talking to you!" Billy said, as if it weren't obvious. He liked to mix up my nicknames. Corny (because of the unfortunate first-day unicorn shirt), Freak. Vamp was a particular favorite as well, as he would claim there was no way someone who wore as much black as I did didn't turn into a bat and bite people's necks during a full moon. (I once tried to tell him the full moon thing was for werewolves—dogs like himself—but he didn't get the insult and eventually I just gave up. It went over much better in my manga.)

"Nothing," I muttered, going back to my drawing. Maybe if I ignored them they'd get bored and go away.

Not today, it seemed. "It doesn't look like nothing," noted Lucy. "It looks like you're drawing something."

"Wow. You got me there," I replied, setting down my paintbrush. "You're amazingly perceptive, Lucy."

"Why do the people in your drawings have such big

eyes?" Chelsea picked up my sketch and gave it a disdainful look. "It's, like, freaky."

"It's Japanese style," I defended, not knowing why I bothered. "That's how they're supposed to look."

"Let me see!" Billy ripped it out of Chelsea's hands. He started laughing. "Wow, you suck, Vamp Girl. And I don't mean blood either."

I'd had enough. "Give it back!" I commanded, rising from my seat to grab my picture. He held it up, beyond my grasp.

"Or what? What are you going to do? Turn me into a toad?" he taunted.

"Please," I begged. "The paint's still wet. You'll smudge it."

The second the words left my mouth I realized I'd made a huge mistake. "Smudge it?" Billy crowed, dragging his fingers down the picture, smearing the art I'd spent hours working on. "I wouldn't want to . . . oops!" he said, giving me a totally fake look of horror. "I think I might've—"

"Give it back!" I cried, lunging at him and punching him full in the face. He bellowed like a little girl, fortunately dropping my picture in the process.

Unfortunately, however, drawing the attention of Mr. Wilks, our science teacher, who, unlike Ms. Reilly, had no sense of coolness whatsoever and didn't appreciate teaching weird girls who refused to model H&M during class.

"What is going on here?" Mr. Wilks demanded.

"The crazy Freak Girl hit me!" Billy cried.

I squeezed my hands into fists, furious and helpless. If I defended myself, we'd just have to go through this again next time Billy caught me alone. It wasn't worth it. Besides, Mr. Wilks was Billy's basketball coach. He thought the kid walked on water. There was no chance in hell he'd believe me over his star.

Sure enough, Mr. Wilks didn't even ask for my side of the story. "Maddy, I don't know about your old school, but here at Hannah Dustin we do not hit our classmates," he clarified, as if I'd been unsure on school policy and had assumed smacking around my fellow students was totally okay with the current administration. "Now go down to the principal's office and explain to him what you did."

I glanced around at the other kids, who'd formed a curious circle around us. I realized no one present was going to defend truth, justice, or the American way. Lucy and Chelsea were smirking in one corner, enjoying the show. Chad stared at his feet, as per usual. There wasn't a soul here who would speak up on my behalf.

"Fine," I retorted, grabbing my comics. I left behind the one Billy had smudged. I'd have to start it all over again anyway. "I'm going."

I made it halfway to the principal's office before bumping into Matt. And I mean literally bumping—like book-dropping and paper-scattering full-on collision. I guess in my rage I hadn't been looking where I was going.

"Whoa, girl, where's the fire?" he asked, bending down to

pick up my books. I crouched down to join him, trying not to get stepped on as I grabbed errant papers.

"Principal's office," I told him, relating what had just happened.

"Ooh, you punched Billy Henderson?" he cried, standing up and handing me my books. I took them gratefully. "It's about time somebody stood up to the guy. Impressive. Very impressive."

"Yeah," I muttered. "Real impressive. It'll be even more impressive when I get to explain to my mom why I've got detention."

Matt waved a hand. "She's got to understand though. I mean, it's not like Billy didn't start it by destroying your painting. He's such a jerk."

I sighed. "No kidding. I spent so long on it, too. Now I'll have to start all over."

"When's it due?"

"Due?" I cocked my head. "What do you mean?"

"Well, I just figured it was like for art class or something."

"Oh, no. I'm creating my own manga."

Matt raised an eyebrow. "Manga?"

"You know, like a Japanese-style graphic novel."

"Yeah, I know what they are. I just . . . You're making your own? Like from scratch?"

"That's the idea."

"Wow, that's heavy-duty." He looked impressed.

"Do you read manga?" I asked curiously. It'd be cool to

find someone here at Hannah Dustin who was into it. Back home my friends and I would hold little impromptu book clubs after school to discuss what we'd read. It started with just Caitlin, Ashley, and me, but then other kids found out about it and would crash our meetings. In fact, it became so popular we'd considered seeing if the school would allow us to form an official club, but then I ended up moving and the idea fell apart.

"Not really, but I'm totally into comic books and have a bookcase full of graphic novels at home."

Huh. Not exactly the same, but close enough. I knew he had friend potential. "Cool," I said. "I like some American comics, too, though I don't know as much about them as I do the Japanese stuff."

"Yeah, well, I'd be happy to bring in some of my favorites if you're interested in checking them out."

"I'd like that. Thanks!"

"There you are!" A tall skinny guy with curly red hair walked up to Matt, hands on his hips. "I've been looking everywhere for you."

Matt grinned at him. "Sorry, I was just helping Maddy with her books." He turned back to me. "You all set now?" he asked. "I've got to go. Luke and I are going to the library to play video games. He's figured out a way to hack into the computers and get by the firewalls they set up."

"Cool," I said, smiling at the two of them. Wow. Comic books and video games. Matt and I had a lot in common. I considered telling him about my Fields of Fantasy adventures, but I was such a gamer noob, I'd probably sound totally poseurish to real gamers like him and Luke. "I need to get to the principal's office anyway before I get in worse trouble."

"Principal's office?" Luke repeated. "What did you do?"

"She punched out Billy Henderson!" Matt said, pride in his voice. At least someone thought I was cool.

"Well, I didn't exactly—"

Luke looked at me with respect. "Very nice," he said.

"Indeed," Matt said, giving me a wink. "Anyway, we'll catch you later, okay? Hope they take it easy on you."

"Thanks," I said. They turned to walk down the hall. I watched them go. Matt was a nice guy. Not boyfriend material exactly. But definitely a new friend. And we all knew how badly I needed one of those.

"HERE, MOM, you have to sign this," I said, dropping off the detention slip on Grandma's kitchen table that evening after school.

"What is it?" she asked, leaving the stove to pick up the note. Her smile faded as she scanned its contents. "Detention? For fighting? Madeline Starr, what's this about?"

I frowned. "Nothing."

"Nothing? A detention is not 'nothing,' young lady. And neither is fighting in school."

Anger welled up inside of me. Of course she'd blame me. She'd never understand that I was provoked and totally justified in my actions. Billy had destroyed my property. My art. Just out of spite. And if I didn't stick up for myself, I was going to be a victim for the rest of the school year.

"It's not *my* fault the kids who go to that stupid school are all stupid jerks with no stupid lives," I muttered, though I was pretty sure my stupid argument wouldn't hold much water with the momster.

Sure enough, she set her lips in a frown. "Madeline, you're generalizing again. I'm sure there are many very nice kids that go to Hannah Dustin."

I screwed up my face. "Yeah, right." Moms were so clueless sometimes.

"Did you ever consider that it's your bad attitude that's scaring them off?" Mom asked. "I mean, maybe if you lost the chip on your shoulder—that 'I hate the world' vibe you walk around with . . ."

I squeezed my hands into fists. "I don't hate the world. The world hates me."

"Well, I simply don't believe that, Madeline. Just because they don't dress like you or act like you doesn't mean they aren't nice people."

"It also doesn't mean they are." I mean, if she was going to go with *that* logic . . .

"Well, you'll never know either way, now will you?" Mom said. "Since you're judging people before giving them half a chance."

"Kind of like how you didn't give *Dad* half a chance?"

Mom's face tightened. I'd struck a low blow. But I was sick of her being so clueless about my situation at school. She had no idea what I had to go through every day. And yet she would, time and time again, insist it was *my* fault I had no friends. As if I wanted to sit alone at lunch and be picked on when I was just trying to learn.

"Go to your room," she said in an oddly calm voice.

"Fine. Gladly." I ran upstairs, taking the steps two at a

time, slamming my bedroom door behind me. I threw myself on my bed, tears coming to my eyes and sobs racking my body. It was so unfair. Life used to be great. I had friends, I had a real family that wasn't split apart. Now what was I left with? Nothing but a broken home and a broken life. I didn't even have anything to look forward to. It wouldn't be until college that I'd have even the remotest chance of bonding with another human being.

If only Mom would forgive Dad for whatever it was he did and get back together with him. We could move back to our old neighborhood. I could return to my old school and be with my friends again.

Yeah, right. So not going to happen. Needed to give up on that fantasy, pronto.

After indulging in a few more moments of self-pity, I glanced over at my computer and then at my clock radio by my bed. It was nearly five o'clock. I was supposed to meet Dad in the Elf Tree Café. Maybe I'd tell him what happened. After all, he was usually a lot more sympathetic than Mom. Maybe if I asked him really nicely he'd figure out a way to pay for me to re-enroll in my old private school.

So I logged on to Fields of Fantasy and selected my character. Allora smiled gleefully, as if she were happy to see me. At least someone was. Too bad that someone didn't really exist.

I gritted my teeth, determined not to let my frustration ruin the game, and sauntered off to the Elf Tree Café. The thatch-roofed bar was cozy and quaint, with wooden benches and tables scattered about, bearskin rugs covering the dirt floor, and a roaring fire blazing in a stone hearth. I sat Allora down by the fire and, on a whim, ordered her a mug of beer from one of the computerized bartenders, hoping Dad didn't choose that moment to walk in. Though in my defense, the drinking age for elves may very well be different from that of Americans. And the bartender *did* serve her without asking for an ID.

I scanned the virtual bar for some sign of my father, but he was nowhere to be seen. Getting impatient, I typed in an instant message to RockStarBob. Maybe he was running late, having had to swing by a troubled village to slay a dragon or something. But my message came back as undeliverable. He wasn't online.

I glanced at my watch. Ten past five. Maybe he got stuck at work. I'd hang out a little longer.

By five-thirty I was about ready to give up. RockStarBob had still not logged on. This was great. My own dad standing me up. Just the ending I needed to my already crappy day. It figured. It just figured.

I started to log out of the game, but then reconsidered. He wasn't going to show up? That didn't mean I shouldn't play. Maybe I'd gain a few levels while I was waiting for him. Then when he did get home, he'd be all impressed by my progress. Besides, what else did I have to do while stuck here in my room waiting for Mom to calm down?

So I guided my character out of the bar and through the town until she reached its gates. A burly computerized guard standing watch warned Allora that she was not yet powerful enough to venture out into the world on her own, but I ignored him. Probably just a scare tactic to get rid of the noobs. Allora knew three spells. She was a tough girl. She could handle herself.

Roar!

Argh! Not three seconds after she'd left the safety of the town, three wolves jumped my poor elf, viciously attacking her, shredding her gown, snapping at her legs. I clicked on her spell book, trying to get off a fire spell to stop them, but they kept interrupting her cast with their snarly, angry bites.

She fell to the ground with a high-pitched scream. Dead.

Luckily since this was just a video game and not real life, her death was only a temporary problem. A moment later, Allora showed up at the town's graveyard, looking all ghostlike. All I had to do, the instructions stated, was run her back to her body and then click a button to resurrect. She'd be as good as new—no big deal.

I did as I was told and sure enough, my pretty elf had soon successfully risen from the dead, just a few feet away from the spot she'd been killed. Problem was, before she could even get her bearings, those nasty, horrible wolves jumped her again, and before I knew it, she was back in the graveyard as a ghost.

I slammed my fist against my desk in frustration, running my hands through my hair. People played this stupid game for fun? It was almost as stressful as school. And a lot more annoying. I tried my dad one more time, praying he'd signed on and could give me some help. After all, he was a higher level—the wolves would pose him no threat, right?

He was still off-line. At five forty-five. I hoped he wasn't in some kind of awful car accident or something. But no, that was stupid. He probably just forgot. Forgot about his promise to me, forgot about me in general. I sighed.

Deciding to give it one last try, I ran back from the grave-yard and hit Resurrect. Sure enough, the wolves pounced on me. It was as if they'd just been hanging out, all rabid, drool-ing, waiting for some juicy elfin flesh to rise from the dead so they could devour her all over again.

Just as I was about to give up and die again, one of the wolves uttered a piercing howl of pain and dropped dead at Allora's feet. The other followed a moment later. My mouth dropped open in surprise. Had I done that somehow? Did Allora have some secret power I didn't know about? The power to—?

[SirLeo] Don't worry. I got 'em.

I stared at the screen. Some random player, whose name I didn't recognize, had just instant messaged me. Was he the one who killed the wolves? I moved the game's camera po-sition around with my mouse so I could take a look. Sure enough, "Sir Leo" stood nearby, lounging against a tree. He was a valiant-looking elfin knight with shoulder-length white hair, blue eyes, and a large sword strapped to his back. Yum. He totally looked just like Legolas.

I realized I should instant message him back and thank him for saving my life.

[Allora] Thanks! They were killing me over and over again!

[SirLeo] LOL. I bet. They're level five. You're level one. Not exactly a fair fight.

[Allora] Yeah. I guess not!

[SirLeo] You shouldn't even be out here in this area at your level. Didn't the guards warn you?

[Allora] Er, they might have. But I kind of ignored them.

[SirLeo] Heh. Well, that explains it then. First day playing FoF?

[Allora] Yeah. That obvious, huh?

[SirLeo] It's okay. You're just lucky I was around to save you.

[Allora] Totally. Thank you so much.

I smiled at the screen, even though he obviously couldn't see my real-life reaction. I was lucky indeed. Lucky to run into such a nice guy. After all, he could have just run off, left me to the wolves. But he stopped to help. Game people sure were nicer than real-life people. At least this guy was.

[SirLeo] So do you want me to show you where you should go? Where the mobs are a bit more your level?

[Allora] Er, mobs?

Sir Leo laughs.

[SirLeo] You really are a noob, huh? Mobs are like monsters. You get quests from the townspeople to fight them and earn experience and treasure.

[Allora] Ah. Cool. Sorry. My dad got me this game and he said he'd show me how to play, but I don't know where he is. He was supposed to sign on like an hour ago.

[SirLeo] Typical dad, huh? Well, I can show you, if you want. This way when he logs in you'll already be totally 1337.

[Allora] 1337?

[SirLeo] Er, like, leet. Short for elite. LOL. Sorry. I'll try to take it easy on you since it's your first day. But don't worry. You'll be a gamer girl in no time.

[Allora] He-he, ty. I appreciate that.

A gamer girl. I liked the sound of that. I also liked chatting with Sir Leo. It was as if I'd just met a new friend. Something I hadn't managed to do in nearly a month of attending Hannah Dustin, I might add. So glad Dad got me the game for my birthday.

[SirLeo] One rule, though.

[Allora] ?

[SirLeo] Don't think this is dorky, but if we're going to adventure together, we've got to role-play.

[Allora] . . . Role-play?

[SirLeo] Yea, like, keep in character. Like, you're actually Allora. You need to give her a personality—what she's like, where she comes from, why she's decided to go adventuring, etc.

[Allora] Oh-kay.

[SirLeo] Hmm. You think I'm a total geek, don't you? ROFL.

[Allora] No! No, not at all. I think it's a kewl idea, actually.

Sir Leo smiles.

[SirLeo] Okay then, let's give it a try.

Sir Leo bows.

[SirLeo] Good evening, young maiden. I fear you may be lost in these here woods? Art thou in need of my assistance, mayhap?

[Allora] Aye, good and noble knight. I am fair happy to make your acquaintance. These wolves have gotten the better of me fair self, I fear.

Sir Leo laughs.

[SirLeo] (Not bad, not bad! You've got the hang of it already.)

[Allora] Hang of what, oh, good noble sir?

[SirLeo] (LOL. You're good! But it's okay to talk out of character if you use parentheses like this. Then I'll know it's you in real life saying something and not your elf.)

[Allora] (Ah, good to know.)

Sir Leo smiles.

[SirLeo] M'lady, art thou new around these yonder parts?

[Allora] Aye, good sir. I am a simple elf orphan whose parents were tragically killed when our town was attacked by wolves. And now I seek nothing in life but to avenge their deaths!

[SirLeo] I see. Well, m'lady, I am a brave and noble elfin knight, sent to this land to claim it for my king. And of course save all the pretty young elf girls who might need rescuing.

Allora blushes.

[SirLeo] (Um, by the way, you're really a girl, right? I mean, in real life?)

[Allora] (Heh. May-be. I guess you can't tell, huh?)

[SirLeo] (Nope. Online you can be anyone.)

[Allora] (LOL. Well, yes, I'm really a girl. Are you really a boy?)

[SirLeo] (Yup.)

[Allora] (You're not like . . . old . . . are you?)

[SirLeo] (Ha-ha. No, I'm sixteen. You?)

[Allora] (Ooh. I'm sixteen, too. Actually I just turned sixteen yesterday.)

[SirLeo] (Really? Happy birthday!!!!!)

[Allora] (He-he, thank you!)

It was so easy to talk to him. Maybe it was the online thing. In real life I was so shy—always worrying that people would judge me when I opened my mouth. But here I could be anyone. Act any way I wanted to. After all, I'd never meet Sir Leo in real life. He probably lived across the country—maybe even across the world.

We chatted a bit more and then I had Allora follow him over to the beginner area, where the monsters were more my level. At first I assumed he'd leave me there and go off to do his own thing, but instead he stayed. And with his help, I was able to gain three levels within fifteen minutes.

"Maddy, I've been calling you for the last ten minutes! What are you doing in there?"

My mom's voice startled me out of the game. I'd been having so much fun with my new friend online that I'd effectively shut out the real world. But now I heard her footsteps padding up the stairs. Great.

"Nothing, Mom," I answered, crossing my fingers she wouldn't barge in.

But it took a lot more magic than mere finger-crossing to keep the momster out. A moment later she was pushing open the bedroom door—Grandma refused to let me get a lock for it!—and staring disapprovingly at my computer.

"Don't you have homework you should be doing?" she asked. "I don't want you up here playing that . . . game." I caught her taking a quick peek at the screen, probably wondering if I was talking to Dad online. Not that she needed to worry about that. He still hadn't signed on.

"No, I did my homework in detention, Mom."

"Detention. Right." Mom sighed. "Turn off the computer. We've got to have a little talk."

I glanced helplessly back at the screen where Sir Leo had just attacked a pack of wolves, not realizing I'd turned away from the computer to talk to Mom. His life was low and he was calling out for me to help him.

"Hang on, Mom. I have to . . ." I turned to the keyboard to finish the fight. I'd save him and then say good-bye. Maybe we could meet later to play more after I got through with Mom.

But before I could launch my fireball spell, my computer screen turned black. "Wha . . . ?" I cried, confused. Then I realized my mom had walked over and hit the computer's Off switch and was currently standing above me with a self-satisfied look on her face. "Mom! I was right in the middle of—"

"When I say turn off the computer, I mean turn off the computer, not continue to play your game," she admonished, walking over to take a seat on my bed.

"But I was helping my friend!" My stomach churned in panic as I stared at the blank screen. This was terrible. Sir Leo had been so nice to me and I'd just up and disappeared without even saying good-bye. The wolves probably killed him and it was all my fault. Great. Now he was never going to want to play with me again. Not that I blamed him. "Can I just log back in and tell him—?"

"No. I came up here to talk to you and I need your full attention," Mom said. "If you're going to become this addicted to the game, I'll take it away altogether."

I swallowed hard, knowing she was perfectly able to make good on the threat.

"Sorry," I muttered. "I'm listening."

Mom nodded. "Look, Maddy. I'm sorry I blew up earlier. When you mentioned your father . . . well, it's a sore subject, as you can imagine."

I stared down at my hands. "Yeah. I know. I shouldn't have said that."

"Sweetie, I know your father and me separating and your

having to switch schools has been really tough on you. It has for all of us. But you can't let it turn you into someone you're not. You're a wonderful girl. Beautiful, smart, creative. Yet all I see these days is someone who's mad at the world and wants revenge. You just can't go around punching other kids, no matter how angry you are at your father."

Argh. I squeezed my hands into fists. So, like everything else, she was going to blame this on Dad. "I'm not angry at Dad," I informed her. "I'm angry at Billy."

"Billy? Who's Billy?" demanded Mom, obviously baffled that anyone could be mad at anyone else in the entire world besides my father.

"The kid I hit, Mom. Try to keep up." I knew I was being bratty, but I couldn't help it. "He destroyed my drawing on purpose. He's a total jerk."

"Why would he destroy your drawing?" She sounded confused. Of course.

"Because he's trying to ruin my life." I squeezed my hands into fists. "You want to know the truth, Mom? No one likes me at school. They all think I'm a freak."

Mom gave my black-dress and black-and-white-striped-tights outfit a look. "Well, I did warn you about dressing that way. . . ."

"Oh, I see. So it's all my fault."

Mom sighed. "No, of course not. But you go to a smaller school now. And kids aren't going to be as diverse as in Boston. But that doesn't mean they're bad people. You've just got to give them a chance. Get to know them. Let them know you. You're a wonderful, beautiful girl. I'm sure in time the other kids will realize that."

"I want to go back to my old school. In Boston."

Mom slumped her shoulders. "Maddy, you know we can't do that. I can't afford it."

"If you just got back together with Dad—"

"Maddy, we've had this discussion."

I wanted to press her further, but I knew it would do no good. "Fine," I relented. "I promise to work harder to make friends. And I won't fight and . . . stuff." I knew my promises sounded flimsy and lame, but I'd say anything at that moment to get out of the lecture.

Mom stared at me for a moment, then shook her head. "Let's talk about this later when we're both less upset, okay?" she said. "It's dinnertime anyway. Grandma cooked a lovely pot roast and I've made my famous green bean casserole."

I glanced longingly back at the computer, wanting nothing more than to log back into the game to find Sir Leo and explain what happened. The last thing I wanted was for him to think I was some total flake who got his character killed. After all, he was my first new friend in forever, even if he was virtual, and I wanted to play with him as much as possible.

But I knew better than to cross Mom when she laid down the law. Better to let her win this round and get back on her good side—even if that did mean digesting Grandma's cooking.

"Pot roast?" I said, smiling my widest, fake smile. "Sounds delish. Let's eat!"

GETTING THREE days of detention stunk. Having detention fall on a Friday stunk worse. Not that I had a hot date or anything. Though I was anxious to get home to log into Fields of Fantasy. I wanted to find Sir Leo online and beg his forgiveness for abandoning him to the wolves the night before.

But I had no choice and so on Friday I sat in Mr. Wilks's otherwise empty classroom, watching the clock tick down the minutes to my freedom. I was supposed to be doing homework, but I just didn't have the energy. And Mr. Wilks made it clear there would be no drawing during detention, so I couldn't even work on my manga.

"Um, Maddy?"

I looked up and my eyes widened as I realized that none other than Chad Murray had walked up to my desk and was actually calling me by name. How did I not notice the god himself wandering into the room? And how did he know my name anyway? I thought I was permanently "Freak Girl" to the Haters.

My heart skipped a beat. He was dressed in a gray T-shirt and a pair of slouchy jeans. He looked gorgeous as always. I mean, if you were into that sort of thing. Which I wasn't. Well, okay, fine, I was still a girl at the end of the day and it was hard not to notice, but it really didn't matter, did it? Chad was one of the Haters. The ones responsible for sticking me in detention to begin with. This Billy lackey was not a guy to have a crush on.

"What do you want?" I demanded, narrowing my eyes. "Come to keep me company?" The sarcasm dripped from my voice. So much for my promise to Mom to be nicer and make friends.

Chad took a step back, as if struck. "Um, nothing, really. It's just . . ." He reached into his book bag and pulled out a piece of paper. He held it out to me. "You left this in the cafeteria."

I looked down at the paper. It was my drawing. The one Billy had destroyed.

"What do I want this for?" I asked. "It's ruined. Your friend Billy made sure of that." Against my better judgment, I smoothed the paper out on my desk, looking at it longingly. My Gamer Girl, Allora, smiled back up at me through the crinkles and paint smears. It had been such a good sketch. . . .

"Right." He shuffled from foot to foot. "But I thought

maybe . . . I don't know . . . you could, like, copy it or something. If you wanted. Then maybe it wouldn't be a total loss."

"Oh." I looked up at him, surprised by the gesture. He really was a lot nicer than his friends. "Yeah, that's not a bad idea. Thanks."

"No prob," he said, still standing there, awkwardly. He paused, then added, "Sorry about Billy. He can be a real jerk sometimes."

"Yeah, just like the rest of the Haters," I muttered, putting the drawing in my bag.

"Haters?"

I blushed. Hadn't meant for him to hear me. "Oh, just a nickname I have for your crew," I explained. "The Haters. You know, since you hate most of the school."

Chad laughed appreciatively. "The Haters," he repeated. "That's funny. And probably pretty accurate, too. I mean, at least for Billy and the girls."

I looked at him skeptically. "And you're different?"

Now it was his turn to blush. "Well, yeah. I mean, I don't mess with people like they do. I hate that kind of thing. I'm more of a live-and-let-live kind of guy."

"So why do you hang with them then?"

He shrugged and looked embarrassed. "I don't know. Billy's been my best friend since kindergarten. I can't just ditch him."

"Right." That made sense. In fact, in a weird way, it was kind of like Caitlin and me. We'd been best friends forever, and when she'd jeer at the Aberzombies and poseurs back at our old school, I'd always laugh, even though sometimes I felt bad for them. Now the tables were turned. Maybe Chad and I were more alike than I realized.

I realized he was still staring at me. "Uh . . ." I tilted my head. "Did you want . . . something else?"

"Actually, yeah," he said. He shoved a hand into his pocket and pulled out another piece of paper. He unfolded it and dropped it on my desk. "I, um, found this in a magazine. I thought, well, your drawings are really good, maybe you'd like to enter or something."

I stared down at the paper. It was a contest for young artists who wrote and drew manga. My eyes widened as I read the rules. Create an original graphic novel and send it in. First prize was publication and ten thousand dollars.

So cool. A chance to have my drawings seen and graded by a professional editor. And if I won—actual publication! My story would be published in a manga magazine. How cool would that be?

Not to mention the cash prize. Ten thousand dollars would be enough for tuition back at my old school. I could go back to my friends and never think of Hannah Dustin High School ever again!

"Thanks," I said, my eyes shining, putting aside for a moment that the contest entry form had been hand delivered by Billy's lackey. "This is really cool."

"No prob," he said with a self-conscious shrug. He ran a hand through his beautiful wavy blond hair. "You should definitely enter. You're really good. The elf totally reminds me of—"

"Chad! Let's go!"

Chad froze in his tracks at Billy's command from out in the hallway. He shot me an apologetic look and backed away.

"Anyway," he said. "I'll, um, see you around."

And with that, he turned tail and ran. I watched him go, shaking my head. Such a waste of cuteness. It was nice of him to tell me about the contest, though. And he said he liked my drawing. That was cool.

But at the end of the day, I knew, none of that mattered. He was and would always be one of the Haters. And thus, would always be the enemy.

I ARRIVED home from detention to a wild, raging party. Okay, it was a wild, raging slumber party for eight-year-olds, but still, the noise level alone should have gotten the cops to the door. Emily and ten other giggling girls were taking up the entire living room, watching a Disney film on Grandma's ancient television. There was a sick amount of food strewn everywhere—pizza, chips, M&M's, chocolate cupcakes. Enough to make all of them go into cardiac sugar shock. Something I hoped happened sooner rather than later so I didn't have to hear the giggles at two a.m. when I was trying to sleep.

"Um, hi, guys," I greeted as I walked into the room. "Having fun?"

Instantly, I had twenty-two eyes fixed on me. They ranged from curious to suspicious to downright annoyed. Emily paused the movie, jumped up from her seat, and marched straight over to me. She folded her skinny little arms across her chest and glared at me with her ice-blue eyes.

"*Mom* said you would stay in your room and wouldn't disturb us," she informed me. "Don't *make* me call her downstairs to remind you."

Nice. After a long day at school and detention, I got to come home and get pushed around by an eight-year-old. "Uh, sure, Em," I retorted, refusing to let her get the best of me. "But let's look at the house layout here for a moment. You see, I *have* to pass through *this* room to get to *my* room. . . ." I paused then added, "I hope that my momentary presence doesn't screw up Your Highness's evening too greatly."

Emily scowled, looking as annoyed as if I had told her I was planning to plop down on the couch and spend the next five hours sharing stories about her thumb-sucking years with all her friends. "Fine. Make it quick," she said, storming back to her seat and grabbing the remote control. She pressed Play and turned up the volume to a nearly deafening level.

Unfortunately the volume didn't drown out the giggles of the other party princesses. Nor did it prevent me from hearing their whispers as I passed through the room, stepping over bowls of popcorn and bags of makeup.

"What's she doing here?"

"Yeah, it's Friday night, way after school. And she's, like, old. Doesn't she have a date or something?"

"Look at her. Who would date her?"

"Dracula?"

"Ooh, ooh, what about Frankenstein?"

Ah, to be judged uncool by a bunch of kids who watched *SpongeBob SquarePants* on a daily basis. Not that they were far off the mark. Though I wasn't sure at this point whether even Frankenstein's monster would consider me a worthy date.

I paused at the other end of the room before heading upstairs. "Have fun," I said in an overly sweet voice. "And don't eat too much or you'll all grow enormously fat and have faces full of zits."

The girls all screamed and gasped.

"Get OUT!" Emily cried, throwing a pillow at me. I easily dodged it and ran upstairs, feeling the tiniest bit better. I entered my room, shut my door, and turned up my stereo, blasting My Chemical Romance's *The Black Parade* album. I'd heard it a gazillion times, but I still loved Gerard's passionate voice. It was as if he totally understood all my pain. If only he went to Hannah Dustin. We'd be soul mates, for sure.

I threw myself down on my bed, exhausted and annoyed. My eight-year-old sister had a full social life and I was a total outcast. So not fair. How did she find it so easy to fit in? To make friends? She would be one of the Haters someday, most likely. Ruling her school with her haughty glare, ridiculing poor innocent people like me for breathing the same air she did.

I glanced over at my computer. Maybe Sir Leo was online. I owed him a major apology after Mom pulled the plug on the game last night. After all, he was the closest thing I had to a developing friendship. I didn't want to lose that.

So I logged on. A few moments later, my character, Allora, smiled up at me. I smiled back at her. "Ready?" I whispered, though of course she couldn't hear me. "Let's go play."

I realized my hands were trembling as I typed in "FIND SIRLEO." I tried to steady them, annoyed. After all, I didn't even know this guy. I'd played with him once. I might never run into him again. And if I did, he would probably be annoyed at me for abandoning him anyway.

CHARACTER NOT ONLINE

I let out the breath I hadn't realized I was holding. Of course he wasn't online. It was Friday night. He was probably on a date with some hot chick who, in real life, looked like my Allora character—not even giving the video game or me a second thought. Virtual life might be all I had to keep me sane, but that didn't mean Sir Leo was as big a loser as I was.

Dad evidently had more of a life than I did as well, as he was not logged on either. So I decided to take Allora adventuring by herself. We headed over to the easy section, where the beginner quests were, and started attacking monsters with her firebombs. It didn't take long until I'd gained another level and was able to get some new, tougher armor and a more powerful magic wand. I also got a new spell—a sort of ice-shield thing that would help protect me. Pretty soon I was strong enough to head out of the town's gates and attack those wolves that had kicked my butt the day before.

"Whoo-hoo!" I cheered as my firebomb blasted them dead. "You go, Allora!"

[SirLeo] Well done, m'lady. I see that the wolves are no longer a trouble to thee.

My heart fluttered with excitement as I read the message sent from Sir Leo. He must have just logged on. Squee!

[Allora] Why, yes. I have been busy learning some powerful new spells to combat the evil wolves that once caused me so much pain.

[SirLeo] I am impressed. Perhaps you would care to join me on a further adventure? There is a small dragon in yonder cave that has been hoarding much treasure. We could slay it and then split the reward.

[Allora] That sounds like a most excellent plan.

[Allora] (By the way, I'm sorry about last night. Mom switched off my computer before I could stop her. Sooo annoying.)

[SirLeo] (Ah, I was wondering what happened to you. I was worried that I'd been boring you to death and you faked a disconnect in order to get rid of me.)

I grimaced. Stupid Mom.

[Allora] (LOL. I've got better manners than that.)

[SirLeo] (So, what, you'd just tell me I was totally boring and I should go away?)

[Allora] (Don't be totally boring and you'll never find out.)

[SirLeo] (LOL. I will do my best!)

Wow. I was flirting. Actually flirting. It wasn't actually so hard to do, safe at home, with a sexy elf as my cover. In real life I'd never be able to talk to a boy like that, but since Sir Leo probably lived on the other side of the country, I had nothing to lose.

> **[SirLeo]** Follow me, my fair and beautiful maiden, and I shall lead thee to thy quest.

I blushed a little at his words. I knew we were just role-playing and that he was keeping in character, but I liked how he flirted back with me all the same. What if he knew how different I looked in real life? Would he be totally turned off? Probably. Which made me kind of sad, actually. I wanted him to like me for the real me, not some fake-o virtual character. But that was stupid and unrealistic. I had to take this for what it was and not get too attached.

> **[Allora]** (Now let's see how long we can play before Mom shows up and starts yelling at me again. If I disappear suddenly, don't take it personally, okay?)
> **[SirLeo]** (LOL! No prob. I know how parents are, trust me.)
> **[Allora]** (Well, my mom used to be okay, before the Big D.)
> **[SirLeo]** (Ah, I went through that two years ago. My mom met this other guy. It was really horrible for a while. All the yelling and screaming. I was almost glad when she moved out and it was just me and Dad again.)
> **[Allora]** (Oh, yeah, the yelling is the worst. I remember all I

wanted to do sometimes was run up to my room and throw the pillows over my head. You know, to drown it all out?)

[SirLeo] (That's how I first got into this game. I could lock myself in my room and play and no one would bug me.)

[Allora] (Makes sense.)

[SirLeo] (Anyway, hang in there. It does get easier.)

[Allora] (Yeah. Well, you obviously didn't have to switch schools.)

[SirLeo] (Oh. You did? That's rough. Though, in a way it must be nice.)

[Allora] ???

[SirLeo] (Well, you get to start over. You can be whoever you want to be. And you get to pick brand-new friends. Anyway, we're at the dragon's cave.)

We found the dragon and between my spells and Sir Leo's sword fighting we totally kicked its scaly butt. As it lay down to die, taking its last fiery breath, Sir Leo gave Allora a big congratulatory hug. Even though it was only a virtual squeeze, I got real-life tingles.

[SirLeo] A most excellent fight, m'lady. Would you like to discover what treasure the dragon has hiding in yonder chest?

[Allora] Oh, yeah!

Allora opens chest.

[Allora] There's a wand in here. A really good one! And a few gems.

Sir Leo bows.

[SirLeo] All yours.

[Allora] Are you sure? I mean, I know you can't use the wand. But these gems . . .

[SirLeo] Please, m'lady, do not insult this knight's honor by refusing his gifts.

[Allora] Cool—I mean . . . lovely. Thank you, good sir knight.

[SirLeo] Now let us take the dragon's head and bring it back to the village, where they are sure to reward our brave deeds.

We started the run back to the village. I swapped out my old crappy wand for the new one I had just gotten from the chest. It had a blue glowing end to it, which totally matched Allora's eyes, not that I was all into elf fashion or anything.

[Allora] (So how come you're home on a Friday night?)

[SirLeo] (I was out earlier, but I have drama practice tomorrow, so I wanted to get a good night's sleep.)

[Allora] (Ah, cool.)

[SirLeo] (How come you're home?)

[Allora] (Oh, uh, I'm not feeling well. So I didn't want to overdo it.)

Okay, so that was a lie. But I didn't want him to think I was some total loser with no friends to hang out with on a Friday night.

Sir Leo frowns.

[SirLeo] I am deeply sorry to hear you are unwell, m'lady. Let us stop at yonder inn and ask the barmaid for some chicken soup before we turn in the quest. Perhaps it will make you feel better.

Allora smiles.

[Allora] Sounds like a plan.

[Allora] Er, I mean that seems like a grand idea, good sir.

Sir Leo laughs.

Yup. A grand idea, indeed. I was feeling better already! I had half a mind to march downstairs and tell those annoying little munchkins that I had a Friday night date after all.

M ADDY, GET up!"

I groaned and pulled the covers over my head. "Five more minutes, Mom."

Mom grabbed the blanket and dragged it off my body. "No. You get up now. Your father will be here in fifteen minutes to take you and Emily to Boston." She looked down at me, an annoyed look on her face. "Why are you so tired, anyway? How late did you stay up last night playing that video game?"

I'd stayed up way too late. Like one-in-the-morning late. But I wasn't about to let her know that. "I don't know. Like . . . nine?" I mumbled.

"Then you should have no problem getting up." Mom headed to the door. "And no falling back asleep once I leave the room either."

I reluctantly sat up in bed, rubbing my eyes. My head felt foggy, my stomach growled. Even my fingers were sore from hours of typing with Sir Leo. And now, instead of getting to sleep in like a normal high schooler on a Saturday morning, I had to get up at the crack of dawn to go visit my dad.

Not that I minded visiting. It meant a weekend back in Boston, in his new apartment. But we always had fun and there was a possibility I'd get to see my friends, too.

Still, the seven a.m. wake-up call was a bit rough. . . .

I forced myself out of bed, glancing longingly at the computer as I passed it on the way to the bathroom. I had such a good time playing last night. Fighting "mobs," completing quests, joking around with Sir Leo—it was awesome. So weird how you could have the best night of your life hanging out with a complete stranger in a virtual world.

When it was finally time to log off and say good night, we'd gone into the Elf Tree Inn. There was only one bed, so Sir Leo gallantly offered it to me and said he would sleep on the floor. Just like a real chivalrous knight! He even blew me a kiss right before he logged off, which let's just say got my real-life heartbeat up quite a bit.

I brushed my teeth and slipped on a black skirt and sweater with black tights and Chinese slippers. Then I grabbed my backpack and headed downstairs, just in time for Dad to walk through the door. He gave me a big bear hug and then turned to Emily, who squirmed and protested he was messing up her hair. My mother hovered in the archway, looking annoyed.

"Hello, Denise," Dad said to her.

"Hello, Bob," she returned in a cold voice.

They used to be so happy together. I remembered sneaking downstairs late at night when I was younger and catching them making out on the couch. Or Dad would be telling some silly joke and Mom would be practically rolling on the floor she was laughing so hard. We'd go on family vacations to the mountains in New Hampshire. Dad would catch us fish and Mom would cook them on the camp stove.

"Hey, how about we all go out for breakfast?" Emily suggested in a bright voice. Poor kid. Still unclear on the concept of divorce. "I'd really love some pancakes. Wouldn't you, Mom?"

Mom shook her head. "I've got a busy day ahead of me, Em. Maybe your father will take you." She started to turn to walk away.

"Aw, come on, Denise," Dad called after her. "You can follow me in your car and we'll meet in the IHOP parking lot." He grinned his goofy dad grin. "You can't be too busy for apple pancakes, can you?"

Mom stiffened. "Yes, Bob. Actually I can be. And, in fact, I am. Some of us work around here, you know."

Ouch. I cringed at her harsh words. It wasn't Dad's fault that he was between jobs after his company laid him off a couple months ago, was it? And besides, he still sent his child-support checks on time, so she had nothing to complain about. She really needed to at least try to be civil to the poor guy. At least around Emily.

"Please, Mom?" Emily pleaded with her big impossible-to-say-no-to eyes. "Please?"

"Can I talk to you for a moment, Bob?" Mom asked, tight-lipped. Dad nodded and followed her to the living room.

"Now you've done it," I remarked, handing Emily her Dora the Explorer suitcase. "You've made them fight again."

"They're talking. That's different," Emily protested. "Dad's convincing Mom to come with us for pancakes."

I rolled my eyes. "Give up the fantasy, girl," I suggested. "They're never getting back together."

Emily's face fell and I instantly felt bad. Still, she needed a reality check. Mom and Dad were done. She'd left him and she was never going back. And we were stuck in this boring town and Grandma's house forever.

Dad walked back into the room with a smile on his face that didn't quite reach his eyes. "Let's go, kids," he said, grabbing our suitcases and pushing open the front door. I looked back to the living room and saw Mom standing in the doorway, her lips pursed in a frown.

Sorry Em, I thought. *As much as it stinks, these two are done for good.*

• • •

After setting my bags in the guest bedroom that Emily and I shared while we were at Dad's, I sprawled on the bed and dug in my purse for my cell phone. I hadn't talked to Caitlin all week. Always got her voice mail every time I dialed and she was never on IM anymore.

"Hello?" my friend answered on the first ring.

"Hey, Cait!"

"Oh, wow, Maddy, how are you? How's the new school? Is it still totally awful? Did you make any new friends? Meet any new guys?"

I smiled into the phone, feeling better already. Maybe I had been imagining her cold shoulder. Maybe things would be all right after all. We could meet up this weekend for coffee and maybe go to the movies. . . .

"School's still annoying. No new friends. Oh, but I got detention for punching someone."

"No way! That rocks." Caitlin sounded impressed. "What'd she do?"

"He, actually."

"Whoa, girl, you punched a guy? You rock my socks!"

"Yeah, well, thanks. Mom is a bit less happy about the whole thing."

"Heh. *Your* mom? I can only imagine. My mom probably would have taken me out for pizza and ice cream to celebrate if I socked some guy for doing me wrong."

I laughed. "Anyway, I'm at Dad's this weekend. What are you up to? Did you want to come by?"

"Uh, well, maybe . . ."

I frowned into the phone. "Maybe?" I questioned. "Did you want to or not? It's not a hard question."

"It's actually, well . . . I'm going snowboarding this afternoon."

"Snowboarding?" I raised an eyebrow. "Since when do you snowboard?"

"Uh, well, I'm just learning. We've got a little club that's been going up every weekend. It's totally fun."

"Club? Who?"

"Oh, a bunch of us. Ashley, Dana, Shantel. You know, the gang."

I did know. Mainly because it used to be my gang.

"I'd invite you along, but there's no room in the car, you know? Too bad, though. David's going to be there."

Yeah, just dig that knife a little deeper, Cait.

"But you should come another time. Ooh, they're here. Gotta go. Later, gator!" Caitlin chimed, sounding way too happy about getting off the phone. I guess I would be, too, if I had David Silverman waiting for me in the car. But still . . .

"Okay. Bye." I hit the End button and dumped the phone on the table. I didn't even know why I was surprised at this point. My friends had clearly forgotten about me.

I pulled out my sketchbook. Guess I should work on my manga for the contest. After all, the deadline was fast approaching and I still hadn't figured out my story line. I examined my sketches with a critical eye. Was I just kidding myself to think that my artwork was prize-worthy? Or was Billy right? Did I completely suck?

I shook my head. Couldn't think like that. Had to stay positive.

I flipped from sketch to sketch, studying each one. I liked the drawings I'd done of Fields of Fantasy Allora, but the ones of me in high school, facing the Haters, weren't bad either. So should I do a reality manga—a shojo set in high school? Or create a fantasy epic with dragons and knights in shining armor? It was a tough choice.

Then inspiration hit me like a lightning bolt. What if a normal high school girl started playing a video game and literally got sucked into the virtual world? Suddenly she was an all-powerful magician, living in a medieval land, instead of the friendless, emo girl she'd been. And she'd have to go on some kind of quest to be able to get home. This way I could combine both story lines and make something that was unique.

I grabbed my pen and started sketching out a few rough scenes. This was going to be so cool.

"Whatcha doing, honey?"

I looked up. Dad was hovering in the bedroom doorway.

"Just drawing," I said, feeling self-conscious all of a sudden. I instinctively put a hand over my drawing, then moved it away. After all, I was entering a contest. I needed to get used to people checking out my art. Still, it seemed weird. Something so personal and private, out on display.

Dad sat down beside me and turned my sketch toward him. "Is this from Fields of Fantasy?" he asked.

I nodded.

"You're really a great artist," he remarked, turning to the next drawings. "I'm very impressed."

I blushed. "You're a dad. You have to say that."

"Really?" He looked up, his eyes twinkling. "Weird, I must have skipped over that part in the dad handbook."

I laughed. Dad always had a way of making me feel good.

"Thanks for the game," I said. "I really love it. I met this awesome guy who's been showing me the ropes and—"

Dad held up a hand. "Hold on a second," he said. "A guy?"

I shrugged. "Yeah. Sir Leo."

"I see. And who is Sir Leo?"

"I don't know. Just some sixteen-year-old kid."

Dad rubbed his chin with his finger and thumb. "I should talk to you about the dangers of online gaming," he mused, half to himself, half to me. "That would be in the dad handbook."

I rolled my eyes. Did he think I was two years old? This was the twenty-first century. We kids were warned about online predators since grade school. "Yeah, yeah, I know," I said. "I'm not stupid."

"If I thought you were stupid, I wouldn't have bought you the game to begin with," Dad replied with a smile. "But I need you to promise me that you will play smart. Even if you feel like you're getting to know some of your online friends, do not give out any personal information to them. Like where you live or go to school. And I mean not ever."

"Okay. Sure. Whatever." I'd heard this lecture a million times, though usually about Facebook and MySpace. Parents were so paranoid about stuff like that. "Anyway, I'm sure the guy lives a million miles away."

"Or he could live right in your backyard. You never know."

I nodded, keeping a poker face, even though the idea of Sir

Leo living in my backyard was extremely appealing. "Right. Well, I promise I'll be careful."

"Cool." Dad rose from his chair, having fulfilled his responsible parent duty of the day. "Well, want to play a bit? I set up a second computer right next to mine in the study. We can adventure together."

I grinned. Finally! "I was hoping you'd say that!"

We headed over to the computers and logged in. I glanced over at Dad's screen. He was a tall, handsome human knight with golden armor and a magnificent white horse. Very fancy compared to the odds and ends Sir Leo wore to battle.

"Cool," I said, impressed. "How'd you get all of that stuff?"

Dad laughed. "A lot of wasted hours playing," he said. He pressed a button and his horse reared and whinnied. "I'll ride over to your village and meet you there."

I logged into Allora and realized she was still lying in the bed I'd left her in. Blushing a bit as I remembered Sir Leo's good-night kiss, I quickly ran her outside the inn and waited for Dad to arrive. I was psyched to be playing with him at last and couldn't wait to see how much his character kicked butt. I looked over to his screen again. Wow, he was level eighty. That must have taken forever to get that high.

"How often do you play, Dad?" I asked curiously.

He shrugged. "I don't know. Whenever I have some free time."

"I'm bored!" Emily moaned, coming up behind us. "Dad, will you play Barbies with me?"

"Not now, sweetie," Dad said, not looking away from the screen as he galloped toward the elfin village Allora lived in. "Why don't you go watch a DVD or something?"

I hid a smile. *Take that, Emily.* It was my turn to hang out with Dad.

Huffing her annoyance at being ignored, Emily retreated to the living room, making a big show of stamping her feet as she left. I turned back to the computer screen. A moment later I saw Dad's character approach on horseback. I glanced over at his screen and saw Allora standing waiting for him. How cool was that? Like looking at yourself with someone else's eyes.

RockStarBob waved at Allora. I made Allora wave back.

"Ready to play?" Dad asked.

I nodded. "Let's go kill stuff!"

Suddenly, a beautiful black-haired woman wandered up to Dad. She was wearing a low-cut dress and carried a very impressive-looking silver staff that sparkled with gems. I watched RockStarBob jump off his horse and give her a hug. The woman winked at him and then blew him a kiss. Evidently they knew each other. Hmm.

[LadyAdriana] Hey, Bob. What are you up to?

[RockStarBob] Nothing much. How are you?

[LadyAdriana] Meh. Ex-husband's giving me trouble again. But what else is new?

RockStarBob gently pats Lady Adriana.

[RockStarBob] Aw. Poor you.

[LadyAdriana]: Thought you'd be stuck with the brats today. Isn't it your turn?

I shot a glance over at Dad. *Brats? Was she talking about Emily and me?* Dad tossed me a sheepish smile. "Sorry," he said. "Lady Adriana doesn't always have the most tact."

"Evidently," I muttered, turning back to my screen.

[RockStarBob] I've got my children with me this weekend, if that's what you mean.
[LadyAdriana] LOL, kk. Listen, I was going to start a raid group. You interested in coming to BlueRock with us if I do?
[RockStarBob] Um, hang on a second.

I felt Dad's eyes on me again. He was obviously trying to judge how upset I'd be if he blew me off for this woman. If he really was "stuck with the brats" today.

"Go ahead," I said with a sigh. I didn't want him to feel like he was forced to entertain me.

"Are you sure?" he asked, looking a little worried. "I mean, I know I said I'd play with you. But I've been dying to do BlueRock for a long time."

I waved a hand. "It's no big deal. I've got a few other quests to do locally anyway."

Dad looked relieved. "Okay, if you're sure. And you can always watch me play. . . ."

"Uh, sure. That would be fun."

Not catching my sarcasm or just choosing to ignore it, Dad turned his attention back to the screen. Back to Lady Adriana. A few minutes later he was completely lost in the game, typing furiously as he rode through the countryside to the BlueRock place.

I stared at the screen, trying to decide if I wanted to log off or play a little anyway. It didn't seem that much fun to play by myself. . . .

[SirLeo] (Yea! You're online. I was hoping you would be.)

I grinned, my heart picking up the pace at the instant message. Sir Leo had just signed in. And he was, unlike everyone else in the known universe, happy to see me!

[Allora] (Woot! Sooo glad you're here. Do you want to quest?)
[SirLeo] (Of course!)
[Allora] (How's your day going?)
[SirLeo] (Good. Just got out of drama practice.)

I tried to picture him onstage, reciting lines. It was tough to form a mental image when I had no clue what the guy looked like in real life. He could be an ugly troll for all I knew. Fifty pounds overweight with a zit-covered face. But for some reason, I didn't think so.

Yeah, he probably pictures you as a six-foot-tall blond elf, too. And we all know how true that fantasy is.

The thought sobered me. What would Sir Leo think of me if he met me in real life? Would he be disappointed? Would he think I was a freak, like everyone else did in my school?

I realized I hadn't typed a response.

[Allora] (Drama? How cool. I always wanted to try it but I think I'd get stage fright.)

[SirLeo] (LOL. Nah, you'd be fine, I'm sure. I mean, you role-play with me. That's very similar.)

[Allora] (It's a lot different typing into a computer than getting up in front of everyone.)

[SirLeo] (I guess. But it's really not as scary as you might think. I mean, you're up there playing a part. A lot easier than being yourself.)

[Allora] (If you say so . . .)

[SirLeo] (I do. And I'm always right, remember?)

[Allora] (LOL. But of course!)

Allora cheers at Sir Leo.

[SirLeo] (I thought you were going to be at your dad's this weekend.)

[Allora] (I am. But he has two computers. He's playing next to me.)

[SirLeo] (Ah, cool. I wish my dad played. He's always working.)

[Allora] (What does he do?)

[SirLeo] (Banker. Fun, fun. How about yours?)

I started to type in my answer, then stopped, remembering Dad's warning. Don't want to give out too much information online.

> [Allora] (Why, he's a knight, of course! Level eighty!)
> [SirLeo] (LOL. Right, of course. Silly me.)
> [Allora] So, my fine sir, art thou ready to go on a quest or two?
> [SirLeo] Indeed, my fair lady, now that you are here by my side.

And so we began questing. And questing and questing. With Dad completely sucked into his own adventures, there was no nagging parent to force me to shut off the computer after an hour or two online. Instead, Sir Leo and I played for hours, side by side, each locked into our own little worlds. Once in a while Emily would wander over, pronounce Dad and me hopeless nerds, then head back to the television.

After a while, Dad was done with BlueRock and he and Lady Adriana started adventuring with Sir Leo and me. With their high level help, we were able to fight bigger monsters and win better treasure. And the whole time the four of us were joking around, teasing one another and generally having a grand old time. I grinned over at Dad and he grinned back at me. He was so much fun. How could Mom not see that? She really needed to lighten up.

"Want to take a break for dinner?" he asked. "Or just get pizza delivery?"

"Pizza delivery." I didn't want to stop questing.

He laughed and hit the number two on his phone's speed dial. Obviously this wasn't the first time he'd made that decision. "I was hoping you'd say that."

"I want french fries and chicken fingers," Emily whined from the next room.

Dad rolled his eyes. "Anything you like, sweetie," he called over to her. He gave me a wink. I winked back.

We continued to play into the night. Before I knew it, I turned level fifteen and had learned some amazing new spells. The wolves that had troubled me my first day were absolutely no threat anymore. In fact, I could kill them in one blow. And I did, too, saving some newbie from certain death and then suggesting he go back and play in the beginner area.

I was beginning to feel like a real gamer girl. Totally 1337—elite—as Sir Leo would say.

Finally, Dad stretched his hands over his head and glanced over to the adjoining living room, where Emily had passed out in front of the television. "I'm going to put her to bed," he told me. "Say good night to your Sir Leo. It's time for you to hit the sack, too."

I looked at the clock, surprised to see it was already midnight. We'd been playing for over eight hours straight! Crazy. Still, I couldn't remember a day in the last year when I'd had as much fun.

"Okay, Dad." I smiled at him. "I'll log off in a minute."

Dad got up to go drag Emily to bed and I turned back to the computer.

[Allora] (It's late. Dad says I have to go to bed.)

[SirLeo] (Yeah. Wow. I didn't even realize it was midnight.)

[Allora] (I know. Time flies when you're having fun.)

Sir Leo smiles.

[SirLeo] (I had a LOT of fun. You're great to play with.)

Allora blushes.

[Allora] (Thanks. ☺ You're fun to play with yourself.)

There was a pause in conversation and at first I thought Sir Leo had left the computer. Then another instant message dinged.

[SirLeo] (Uh, sorry. I was just . . .)

[Allora] (??)

[SirLeo] (Well, it's weird to play with you so much and not know anything about you. I mean, I know you probably live on the East Coast, because we're in the same time zone. But besides that . . .)

[Allora] (Yeah. It is weird. I feel like I know you really, really well, and yet not at all.)

[SirLeo] (Yes! It's crazy. At least tell me where you live.)

I swallowed hard, my hands hovering over the keys, not sure what to do. Dad had just warned me about this. And I'd laughed him off, saying I'd never do it. And yet here I was, a few hours later, totally tempted.

[Allora] (Um, I'm not supposed to say. Dad's rules, remember?)

Argh. Even as I typed it, I realized how stupid I sounded. How babyish. Sir Leo was going to think I was a total loser. Either that or I was completely uninterested in him, which was so not the case. Heck, if there was any way in the known universe to meet him in real life, I would in a heartbeat.

[SirLeo] (Oh. Right. Yeah, that makes sense. Your dad's smart. I mean, you never know. Not that I would do anything, obviously. But how would you know that?)
[Allora] (Right. I mean, I don't know you. Well, not the real you, you know?)

Wow, this was awkward and I wasn't explaining myself very well. The last thing I wanted was for him to think I didn't trust him.

[SirLeo] (Sorry, I shouldn't have even asked. My bad.)
[Allora] (It's okay. Don't worry about it.)
[SirLeo] (It's just . . . well, I think you're really cool. And I know you probably still live a thousand miles away and would never want to anyway, but I just can't help thinking how awesome it'd be to meet you in real life.)

I stared at the computer, too dumbfounded to type a reply. He wanted to meet me? In real life? I suddenly felt faint and my stomach started flip-flopping as I imagined the scene playing out. Sir Leo, stepping into the room, handsome and breathtaking. Breaking into a big smile as his eyes fell on me.

Me, grinning back at him, my heart beating a mile a minute. Him, sweeping me up into a tender embrace and kissing me senseless.

I shook my head. *Fantasize much, Maddy?*

Before I could type a reply, Dad burst back into the room. "Did you say your good nights?" he asked, walking over to the computer. Quickly, I minimized the game screen, red-faced, not wanting him to read our conversation. Seeing a guy online say he wanted to meet me in real life was so going to set off the parental warning bells.

"Um, yeah," I stammered. "I'm just going to check my e-mail and go to bed."

Dad kissed the top of my forehead. "Okay, sweetie," he said. "I'm going to brush my teeth and hit the hay. See you in the morning." He exited the room.

Once alone, I maximized the game screen again. In my absence, Sir Leo had continued typing, probably assuming I was too shocked to answer him. I scanned the chat screen, cringing at what I'd missed.

[**SirLeo**] (Um, I can't believe I just typed that. Never mind. Forget I said anything.)

[**SirLeo**] (This is stupid. You're probably not even a real girl or something.)

[**SirLeo**] (I mean, not that I don't believe you or anything. Sorry, that came out wrong.)

[**SirLeo**] (Um, hello? Are you there?)

[**SirLeo**] (Great. I probably scared you off. I'm sorry.)

Sir Leo sighs.

[SirLeo] (Well, good night. It was fun playing with you. Sweet dreams.)

Sir Leo logs off.

I banged my head on the desk in frustration. What had I just done? Probably completely embarrassed him and made him think I wasn't interested. Which was so not the case. In fact, I had a raging, burning, out-of-control crush on the guy.

But what choice did I have? I tried to rationalize. Even forgetting that whole online safety thing for a moment, did I really want to meet him in real life? I mean, he thought I was a beautiful elf chick. If he met the real Madeline Starr, he'd probably run screaming in the other direction.

I switched off the computer and got up from my chair. It was better this way, I told myself. Be online friends and leave it at that.

So why did that seem so hard to do?

10

THE REST of the weekend passed uneventfully. On Sunday, Emily staged an anti-video-game protest that threatened to turn violent if we dared log on for even the slightest moment just to check our in-game mail. So Dad gave in to her demands, packed up some Cokes, and together we headed downtown to the cinema.

"One for each of you," he explained, pressing the tickets into our palms. "Just to get past the ushers. Then we can movie-hop all day long. Oh, and Maddy," he added, "I got you a child's ticket. If anyone asks, you need to tell them that you're eleven, okay?"

"Okay," I said reluctantly. "Whatever." Dad was weird like that. He'd drop a thousand dollars on a souped-up computer without thinking twice, but totally balk at spending a couple extra dollars on an adult movie ticket for his teenage daughter. I think he liked the idea of feeling like he was getting away with something. He winked at me as we handed over our tickets to a zit-faced, bored usher—who would have probably let me in if I'd insisted I was an eighty-three-year-old grandma—and then high-fived me as I officially entered into the inner sanctum of the AMC.

"Nice job, Maddy," he praised. "Way to stick it to the man."

I didn't know who he considered the "man" in this scenario. (It couldn't be the usher!) But I did reluctantly admit to myself, not for the first time, that Mom could be onto something with her whole "your dad never grew up" theory.

We watched three movies in a row. I slept through most of the last one, bored out of my mind. All I wanted to do was to go home and play Fields of Fantasy with Sir Leo. I wondered if he'd logged on this afternoon. If he was playing right this very second. If he missed me and wondered where I was. I hoped he didn't think I was avoiding him after our convo last night. . . .

I sighed, shoveling a handful from my third bag of popcorn in my mouth. *"Free refills!"* Dad had said when he bought the large. *"Fill up and we won't have to eat dinner!"* I'd just have to log in the second I got home. Straighten things out between us. After all, Sir Leo's friendship was about the only good thing happening in my life right now. The last thing I needed was to screw that up, too.

• • •

Dad dropped us off around six. Mom had cooked a three course meal that both Emily and I were too full to eat, thanks

to about fifteen buckets of extra-buttered popcorn, three giant bags of M&M's, and at least a gallon of Coke. When questioned, Dad swore we had hit the all-you-can-eat salad bar
on the way home and Emily and I were just too stuffed with
wholesome lettucey goodness to eat another bite.

I could tell Mom didn't believe him for one second, even
when Emily and I grunted confirmations to his outrageous
lie, just so they wouldn't start fighting again. Dad made a
quick exit out the door and I headed upstairs, despite pleas
from Mom that I come watch the latest and greatest episode
of some random NBC drama or other that she had become
addicted to. Three movies in a row had already put me over
my limit for passive, mindless media. I needed something in-
teractive to excite my weary brain.

I needed Fields of Fantasy.

Or—because who was I fooling, really?—I needed Sir Leo.

I shut my door, blocking out the real world, and sat down
at my computer, ready to immerse myself in the life I was already starting to prefer. The one where parents didn't lie and
fight. Where friends didn't let me down. Where bullies didn't
torture me. And where I could hang with the guy who was
fast becoming my best friend.

If he wasn't mad at me.

Allora smiled as she appeared on the screen, as if she
were happy to be back online. A blinking message told me I
had new mail. I walked her over to the mailbox outside the
inn and took a look.

Allora,

Hope you didn't get annoyed at me asking you all those questions yesterday. I guess it's just that I think you're really cool and I was curious about the real-life you. But I totally understand what your dad says about not giving out personal info on the Web. It's smart really. And there's no way for me to prove that I really am who I say I am. Anyway, I hope we can still play and you're not mad at me 'cause I think you rock.

Also, your magic comes in wayyy handy with the dragons and stuff. lolz. jk. (Sorta.)

Love,

Sir Leo

I could feel the smile spreading across my face, the annoyances of the day fading into oblivion. He was so sweet. So, so sweet. I reread the note, tingles pricking all the way down to my toes. He liked me. He really, really liked me. He even signed his note with LOVE!

SQUEE!

I checked to see if he was online. No luck. Guess I'd have to just write him back.

Dear Sir Leo,

It's all good. I totally still want to hang out and play. Sorry about last night. . . . Actually, I only closed the screen because my dad came by and he'd have gotten really mad if he saw me talking to someone about real-life stuff after he told me not to. He's real anal like that. Anyway, I still want to play as much as possible coz I <3 this game and you're totally fun to play with. (Not to mention you're a great tank—little cloth-robed me would totally be smooshed without you!! He-he.)

I paused, trying to decide how to end the note. Then, deciding to be daring, I signed "XOXOXO" and then Allora. After all, he signed "love" first. Then I hit Send before I could chicken out and delete them again.

Because even if, for necessary reasons, the guy who played Sir Leo couldn't be my real-life boyfriend, there was no harm, no foul, for Sir Leo to be hooking up with Allora online, was there?

I REPORTED to my final day of detention only to have Mr. Wilks tell me that he had a family emergency and couldn't stay to babysit me, so I was off the hook. Problem was, by the time he told me, the first bus had already left, so I was still stuck at school for an extra hour, even if I didn't have to spend it in his classroom. Mom was at work, so I couldn't call her for a ride and there was no way I was going to ask Grandma—I didn't want a repeat of her last visit to Hannah Dustin.

So I wandered down the halls, wondering how to occupy myself. It was then that I noticed the doors to the school theater were open. Curious, I peeked in. The lights onstage were up full and the drama kids were rehearsing. Suddenly, Chad Murray entered stage left, wearing a belted tunic and carrying a sword. I grinned involuntarily. Chad in tights. Delish.

Yes, I still hadn't been able to shake my crush. Especially after he'd gone out of his way to return my drawing last week. He really was a nice guy, no matter who he hung with. And smart, too—I'd noticed he was always acing tests in class. And though he rarely raised his hand, when the teacher called on him he always had something interesting to say. Totally unlike the rest of the Haters, who were self-absorbed idiots who saw school as a platform to enhance their small town celebrity status, rather than a house of learning.

I sighed. If only there was a way to get to know him better. But whenever I saw him, he was glued to Billy's side. And that made him permanently off-limits. Not to mention he was way out of my league. I'd seen the beautiful girls who threw themselves at him on a daily basis. If he didn't go for them, there was no way he'd ever go for me.

But that didn't mean I couldn't spy from afar. So I propped my knees against the chair in front of me and got comfortable, pulling out my sketchbook. Maybe I could get some inspiration for my manga for the in-game scenes. After all, they were performing the Arthurian play *Camelot* and so there was a definite medieval theme going on, similar to the elfin kingdom in my book.

As I turned my attention to the stage, I saw Chad/Lancelot falling to his knees in front of the fair maiden playing Guenevere, (aka Sarah Silver from my B-period history class), taking her hand in his. He looked up at her, transforming from high school student to beautiful knight beseeching his lady queen.

"Genny," he said, in an English-accented voice. "I love you. Lord forgive me, but I do."

I squirmed in my seat, his words sending delicious tingles

down to my toes. Funny, it was kind of like how I imagined Sir Leo would talk, if he were real. That formal English speech, his voice, rich and almost majestic. I closed my eyes for a moment, my mind, in fantasy overdrive, imagining Chad, on his knees, whispering those words to me.

"Then Lord forgive us both," Sarah/Guenevere cried, pulling me out of my daydream as she pulled the knight actor to his feet. They paused for a moment, locking eyes on each other, then Chad slowly took her face in his hands and pressed his mouth against hers.

A pang of jealousy stabbed at my gut and I watched them lock lips. So unfair.

They kissed for only a moment, then broke away to continue the scene. I watched, impressed. Chad was good. Really good. Up there onstage he seemed like a different person from the one that hung out with Billy and the Haters. More confident, more sure of himself. He wasn't shuffling and stammering like he normally did. He was in his element here, I guessed. Just like I was when I pulled out my sketchbook and drew.

The scene ended and Mr. Seifert, the drama coach, stood up from his seat in the front row. "Okay, take five," he said. "Chad and Sarah, good work. Keep it up."

The houselights came up, flooding the room and raising my low profile by quite a bit. Embarrassed at being caught lurking, I jumped up from my seat and started heading for the door.

"Maddy, wait!"

Busted. I froze. Someone was calling me from down by

the stage. Someone that sounded suspiciously like Chad. My heart started pounding my chest and I realized my hands were shaking. I shoved them behind my back as I turned around. He ran up the aisle and stopped in front of me.

"Yes?" I asked, cool, calm, and collected. Well, sort of.

He stared at me, as if he'd forgotten why he had called out to me. He ran a hand through his tousled blond hair and I noticed his cheeks were all flushed—probably from running after me. Surely he wasn't blushing. . . .

"How's . . . how's your manga coming?" he asked. "Did you decide to enter that contest?"

"Oh!" I was surprised at his question. "Actually, yeah. I did. I figured out a great story line for it and I've just been sketching out the scenes. It's sort of half fantasy and half real life. I'm calling it *Gamer Girl* and . . ."

I trailed off. What was wrong with me? Why was I babbling about my manga? As if he cared what it was about. Sure, he asked, but he was probably just being polite. And here I was rambling on and on like a total geek. Stupid, Maddy, really stupid.

"Cool title," Chad remarked, smiling at me. "So what's the story line?"

"W-well," I stammered. I couldn't believe he actually sounded interested. "It's about this girl who starts playing this video game and then gets sucked into the virtual world. She, like, becomes her game character and has to use her new powers to—"

"Maddy!" Matt called out from down the aisle. I forgot

that he was a drama geek, too. I swallowed down my annoyance at the interruption. After all, he had no idea of my crush on Chad or how long I'd wanted to have a conversation with the guy. Still, he had the worst timing ever!

"Hey, Matt," I said, giving him a small wave. I turned back to Chad. "So, yeah, she has to figure out how to get home and—"

"Did you watch our scene?" Matt butted in again as he reached us. I seriously wanted to kill him. "What did you think? Do you have any interest in trying out? We're still casting a few of the minor roles."

I shook my head. "No way. I'm so not an actress." Something inside reminded me about role-playing with Sir Leo, but I dismissed it. That was different. In private and not in front of an audience. And in any case, with my popularity level at Hannah Dustin, I'd probably get rotten tomatoes thrown at me on opening night, even if I did manage to give a Tony-worthy performance. "But, yeah, I thought you guys rocked up there." I turned to Chad. "You were really good," I told him.

Chad blushed, staring down at his feet. "Thanks," he said. "I live for this stuff."

I studied his beautiful face. "You really like it, huh? Acting, I mean?"

He nodded. "When I'm up there, onstage . . . it's just a powerful feeling, you know? It's like I can be anyone."

"I can see that. . . ."

"Have you never been up onstage before?" Matt blurted

out, obviously still not getting that this was an A/B conversation and he should be C'ing his way out of it. Grrr.

I thought about it for a moment. "No, unless you count the time I was the baby Jesus understudy my first Christmas. . . ."

Matt snorted. "Um, no it doesn't count." He reached out and grabbed my hand, dragging me away from Chad. "Come on. It's high time you tried."

"Oh, no." I dug my heels in. "No, no, no, no." One, I wanted to finish my convo with Chad. And two, I had absolutely zero desire to go up onstage in front of everyone.

He grinned wickedly. "Come on. Just for a sec."

I sighed. I was not going to win this fight. I could feel Chad's eyes on me as Matt pulled me onstage. Great, not only would I be stuck up here with Matt, but Chad would be watching my sure-to-be-pitiful performance. How embarrassing.

"Um, now what?" I asked, feeling lame and stupid. The lights blinded me and I couldn't see out into the auditorium without squinting. At the same time I could feel all the stares from the drama club members. Probably wondering what Freak Girl would do next.

"Okay, so you be Guenevere and I'll be Lancelot. I'm actually Chad's understudy," Matt explained. He dropped his voice. "Even though I'm so much better than him, you know."

Sure he was. "Um, okay. But I don't really get what you want me to do."

"Just follow my lead." Matt grabbed my hands, then dropped to his knees and looked up at me with his typical overdramatic flair. "Genny," he cried. "I love you. Lord forgive me, but I do," he recited.

Yuck. He was terrible. And the lines sounded so different when they came from Chad. With Chad I got tingles down to my toes—even sitting out in the audience. Matt was less than a foot away and might as well be reciting a grocery list for all he did for me.

"Come on, Actress Girl, say your line!" Matt hissed up at me.

"Oh, ah." I racked my brain, trying to remember Guenevere's line. "Then Lord forgive us both!" I muttered, worry fluttering through my stomach as I remembered what came next.

Matt rose to his feet. He wasn't going to kiss me, was he? I glanced offstage at Chad, who was still watching me, a strange expression on his face. If only he were up here, holding my hands, pressing his lips against mine. I'd have been seeing rainbows and starbursts and fireworks for sure!

But Matt? While he seemed like a cool guy and had started to become a friend, he was still so not my type. And the last thing I wanted to do was kiss him.

Luckily, it appeared Matt wasn't all that comfortable locking lips with me either. Instead, we both stared awkwardly at each other and I wondered what we were supposed to do next. I was so over this acting thing at this point (not that I was ever into it to begin with) and wanted nothing more than to run offstage and out of the auditorium altogether, never to return.

Or at least hang out and continue my conversation with Chad.

A clapping and wooting broke me out of my trance. Relieved, I jumped back, putting as much space between Matt and me as possible. I looked out into the audience to see who had interrupted us.

Ah, it was Billy. Of course.

"Wow, Matt. You're quite the actor," Billy said, walking slowly to the stage, still clapping. "To make it look like you were actually attracted to Freak Girl. That must take mad skills, man. I mean just look at her! Are there any trolls in this play? She'd be perfect."

I could hear the snickering from backstage from the rest of the actors. Oh, yes, hardy-har-har. No one would possibly be attracted to me.

I waited a beat, wondering if anyone (read: Chad) would stick up for me. Defend my honor as the real Lancelot du Lac would have done for his lady Guenevere.

But no. Heaven forbid anyone in this forsaken school should stand up to the great and wonderful Billy Henderson. Chad might have been sweet and nice and interested in my manga, but at the end of the day, he was still as spineless as ever.

"I'm out of here," I muttered, pushing past Matt and stomping offstage. My face burned in fury and embarrassment. I was such an idiot. I mean, what had I been thinking, going up onstage like that? Was I really that much of a glutton for punishment?

"Aw, where are you going, Freak Girl!" Billy jeered.

I heard Matt calling my name as I dodged props and lighting equipment, heading for the backstage door, but I ignored him. All I wanted to do was get the hell out as quickly as possible. I never should have invaded drama club to begin with.

I retreated to an empty classroom and sank down into a chair, head in my hands. This was just what I needed to knock me back to Earth after what turned out to be a pretty decent weekend, all things considered. Soon after I'd sent Sir Leo my note, he'd logged into the game and we'd stayed up way too late doing this quest where you had to collect ingredients to make a special stew. Not the most exciting quest in the universe and it involved a lot of brainless button mashing, but we'd made it fun—chatting, joking, flirting throughout. When we'd finally finished and sat eating our stews by the raging fire in the Elf Tree Inn hearth, I looked up at the clock and was shocked to see it was past midnight, real-life time. Time flew when you were adventuring with Sir Leo.

But now the elf princess had turned into a pumpkin. Prince Charming had faded into the virtual night. Reality had set back in. I felt like crying, but I was too proud to allow the tears to fall. I was so sick of being a victim. Of letting Billy and the rest of them torment me and make my life hell. If you'd have told me last year this was the person I'd become, I probably wouldn't have believed you. And now, a year later, I could barely remember the girl I used to be. The life I used to lead. Hanging with friends, going to movies, trying on clothes, giggling about boys. Being myself without worrying about being judged for it. It was almost as if that were someone else's life. A movie I once saw.

A janitor came by and kicked me out of the classroom, so I wandered into the library and sank down into a chair. I pulled out my sketchbook and looked down at the picture of Sir Leo I'd drawn. Funny how he'd taken on a lot of the physical characteristics of Chad. Beautiful but unattainable Chad. I traced a finger over the character's face. If only I could become like my heroine and get sucked into a video game and meet a dashing knight. I'd be much happier in there than in the real world, I was sure.

A girl I didn't recognize entered the library. Redheaded, skinny, with a face full of freckles. She sat down a few tables away near the door and I watched, surprised, as she pulled a copy of *Sojo Beat* out of her book bag and started poring over the stories inside. My eyes widened in excitement. A fellow manga lover! Who would have thought they existed at Hannah Dustin High? I wondered if I should go over and introduce myself. Would she think that was weird?

I realized I had to take a chance. Otherwise I was doomed to be friendless Freak Girl for the rest of the year. So drawing in a breath, I rose from my seat and walked over to her table. She looked up at me expectantly and I suddenly felt awkward, not sure what to say. Half of me wanted to run the other direction, but I planted my feet firmly on the ground and forced myself to speak.

"Um, hi," I stammered. "I'm Maddy. I noticed you have the latest issue of *Sojo Beat*. I haven't gotten mine yet. How is it?"

"Oh, it's so good," she exclaimed, her eyes shining. "There's an awesome bonus Vampire Knight this month. I just love Vampire Knight, don't you? Yuki is the coolest girl ever. I wish I could be her. Then I could hang out with Kaname. How cool would that be?"

I laughed. "Pretty much the coolest thing ever," I agreed. "He's so dreamy."

"I'm Sarah," she said, throwing me a grin. "I don't think I've seen you around."

"I'm Maddy. I just moved here a few months ago."

"Cool. Where did you come from?"

"Boston."

"Oh, the city. Nice. You must hate it here. It's so boring."

"It's okay," I said with a shrug. Didn't want to come off like a big-city snob to my potential new friend.

A car pulled up outside the library doors and beeped. Sarah looked over and waved. "That's my mom," she said apologetically as she gathered up her books. "Gotta go. It was nice to meet you though. Always looking for more manga fans."

"Are there others?" I asked curiously. "Here at Hannah Dustin, I mean."

"Oh, sure, there's tons. Not everyone brings their books

to school like I do. But, yeah, there are lots of kids into it."
The car outside beeped again. "Okay, she's ready to kill me."
She laughed. "I'll catch you around."

I watched as she skipped through the library and pushed
open the glass doors, exiting the building. How lucky that I
ran into her. A manga fan. And she said there were others,
too. Who would have thought? It would be great if we could
get everyone together. Maybe do a manga club like Caitlin
and I had back in Boston. And this time I could make it
official. Just like we'd always wanted to. I wondered how
you started up something like that. I guess I'd have to ask a
teacher. Maybe Ms. Reilly. She was into manga. . . .

What was I thinking? I shook my head. This wasn't like
Boston. No one at Hannah Dustin was going to join a club
run by Freak Girl. I'd end up sitting at that first meeting
alone in an empty classroom, praying someone—anyone—
would show up, avoiding the pity in Ms. Reilly's eyes when
she realized no one was coming. It'd be humiliating, embarrassing, and an utter failure.

Unless it wasn't, a small voice inside me encouraged. After
all, Matt would probably join; he liked comics. And maybe
Luke, if Matt could tear him away from his video games. And
that girl Sarah I just met would probably show up. And she
might bring some of her friends. She did say she knew others
who liked manga. . . .

I squared my shoulders and firmed my resolve, deciding
to go for it. After all, what did I have to lose? I already had no
friends and no life—if it didn't work I wouldn't be any worse

off than I was now. And if it was successful? I'd have a whole score of potential new friends.

Excited, I grabbed my stuff and headed down the hall to Ms. Reilly's classroom, crossing my fingers she hadn't left for the day. But my luck held. She was at her desk, working, when I walked in.

"Hey, Ms. Reilly."

She looked up. "Maddy!" she said, smiling at me. "You're here late."

"Yeah, just waiting for the second bus," I said. "Mr. Wilks let me out of detention early 'cause of some family thing."

Ms. Reilly did a double take. "Detention?" she asked. "Why would you have detention?"

I sighed. I knew I shouldn't have brought it up. But then again, she did say I could come talk to her. And honestly I was getting pretty sick of holding everything inside. "I, um, got into a fight with Billy Henderson." I explained what happened, with him destroying my painting. "I was so mad," I said, feeling a lump in my throat as I relived the memory. "I just kind of lost it. Not very cool, I know."

Ms. Reilly looked at me with sympathy. "Ugh," she said. "You've had a rough time since you moved here, haven't you?"

"Yeah, it hasn't been great," I admitted.

"Believe me, I know what it's like," she said. She yanked out her hair elastic and red curls tumbled around her shoulders. It suddenly dawned on me that she wasn't very much older than the kids she taught. Twenty-two, twenty-three maybe?

"Growing up, I was what they called an army brat," she said, placing her black-rimmed glasses on the desk. "My dad was in the navy and we moved around every year. And that meant every year I had to start a new school in some other city and state. I was shy and bookwormy back then and wore really thick glasses to correct my nearsightedness. Let's just say I wasn't exactly the most popular kid in any of my schools. In fact, it was downright near impossible for me to make friends. And then if by some miracle I managed to find a kindred spirit or two at a particular school, Dad would inevitably announce we were moving again." She shook her head. "I'd try to stay in contact with my old friends—the ones who were so difficult to make in the first place—but it was always out of sight, out of mind. Once I'd moved away, they forgot about me, just like that. It was as if I never even existed."

"I know the feeling," I muttered against my will. I thought about the early mornings before the first bell rang. The lonely lunches by myself in the back of the cafeteria. It wasn't a pretty picture. "I used to like high school. Now I'd rather get drilled at the dentist."

Ms. Reilly laughed appreciatively. Then she turned serious. "Look, I know it's hard to imagine there's life after high school, Maddy. But trust me, it gets better," she promised. "For people like me and you, it really, really gets better."

I wanted to dismiss her words as teacher talk. As an after-school special gone bad. But there was something about the way she spoke. The look in her eyes. She really believed what she was saying.

"Easy for me to say, right?" she asked with a small smile. "But hard to do."

I nodded. "Right. I mean, it's not like I'm asking to be picked on. I don't do anything to them."

"Right. You're just an easy target. Gotta stop that."

I frowned. "What am I supposed to do?" I growled. "Just run around and pretend like it doesn't bother me?"

"No. Pretending isn't enough. You've got to get to the point where it really *doesn't* bother you. Stop giving them your power."

I cocked my head. "Huh?"

"By letting them upset you—by reacting—you're giving away your power. You're letting *them* and other outside things control your happiness. You need to figure out a way to be happy in here." She placed a hand over her heart. "And then what happens out here"—she waved around the room—"won't bother you so much anymore."

I nodded slowly. Okay, so it was total psychobabble, but what she said made sense, in a weird way. Why should the Haters get to decide if I had a good day or bad day? They meant nothing in the grand scheme of life. Just lame kids in a dinky little suburban town. High school would be the peak of their pathetic lives, whereas I had bigger plans for mine. Like becoming a famous manga artist for one. Which reminded me of my reason for coming here to begin with.

"Actually, I had this idea," I said slowly, crossing my fingers she'd be receptive to it. "I was wondering how someone would start a school club."

She cocked her head. "What kind of club?"

I took a deep breath. "A manga club. I was talking to this freshman and she said there were a lot of people in school that read it here. I thought we could maybe get them all together. Meet after school and read books and watch anime."

Ms. Reilly nodded slowly, thinking it over. "That's not a bad idea," she mused. "The principal's been asking me to come up with some sort of book club for some time now—they want kids to learn to love reading, you know. So I really don't see any problems with something like this getting fast-tracked approval."

"I mean, I don't know how many people would show up," I hedged. "I mean, this place is pretty Aberzombie. I'm not sure we've got a lot of closet cosplayers waiting to embrace their inner InuYasha."

Ms. Reilly laughed appreciatively. "Sure, I doubt Billy Henderson would suddenly show up to school sporting dog ears, but I do believe there are a good number of students who would really appreciate this kind of thing. After all, there's certainly nothing else like it right now."

"So how do we get started?"

"Well, I'd have to go get permission from the administration before we would be able to officially announce it. Have to get the official go-ahead, you know. But I don't see it being a problem."

"Awesome." I grinned. Suddenly things were looking up. Way up.

"By the way," Ms. Reilly said with a smile, "you never did show me your art."

"Oh." I felt my face heat. I wasn't sure I wanted to show her. What if she thought my sketches weren't good? I mean, this wasn't like showing my family. Ms. Reilly had obviously seen her fair share of real manga. What if she thought my drawings were totally amateur?

Then again, I was entering the contest. And I had to get used to showing my work to people sooner or later. Might as well start with someone nice.

"Okay," I agreed, reaching into my book bag and pulling out my sketchbook. I handed it over to her and she flipped it open. She turned a few pages, looking at each one closely before moving on to the next. Her expression was blank. Unreadable. I held my breath.

"Wow," she said suddenly, looking up after coming to the last page. "And here I had thought I was going to have to make up some encouraging teacherlike compliment. But your stuff is actually good. I love it."

I could feel my cheeks heat. Was she being serious? I studied her face. She certainly looked like it. "Thanks," I said shyly. "It's sort of my passion."

"This is really great stuff, Maddy. Better than some of the published manga I've seen," she continued. "Your style and subject matter reminds me of this game I know. Ever hear of something called Fields of Fantasy?"

"You play Fields of Fantasy?" I sputtered.

She laughed. "No, no," she said, shaking her head. "I'm

not that cool. My boyfriend's addicted to it, though. He plays twenty-four/seven. In fact, it's impossible to drag him away for a date sometimes."

"Heh. He sounds like my dad. He's the one who introduced me to the game. Well, he bought it for me. But he's a lot higher level, so we haven't played together much."

"Yeah, I know that song and dance," Ms. Reilly replied. "Tim's constantly trying to get me to play, but he'd never actually lower himself to play with me at my piddly level."

"Right." I nodded.

"Boys," she said, sounding amused. "But in any case, those are great sketches."

"I hope so. I'm entering a contest." Might as well show her, right? I pulled out the flyer from my bag, smoothed it out, then handed it to her. She studied it a moment, then passed it back to me.

"Nice," she said. "Cool prizes." She looked down at my sketchbook. "I bet you have a good chance, too."

"Thanks," I said, feeling the blush creep over my cheeks again.

"It's not a compliment. Simply a fact."

I grinned. Another fact? She was the coolest teacher ever. And things at Hannah Dustin were really looking up.

ONCE HOME, I informed Grandma that I wasn't hungry, endured a lecture on the growing menace of teenage anorexia, then escaped to my room. Once secured in my sanctuary, I opened up my sketchbook and started drawing.

I'd settled on my story line and now was creating the initial scenes. As I was telling Chad in the auditorium, the premise was pretty simple. Allora, my gamer girl, gets sucked into her video game for the first time and is transformed from regular outcast high school student to popular elfin princess with magical powers to take down enemies with a mere snap of her fingers and a wave of her wand. (If only she had these powers back in high school, things would be a lot easier when facing the bullies.) But though she likes being all-powerful and enjoys the medieval world where she's loved and adored, she misses her family back on Earth.

So she consults with the wise man of her village, who tells her she must go on a dangerous journey to recover a special potion with the power to send her home. As she begins her quest, she runs into a handsome knight in shining armor—Sir Leo—who says he will help her. She doesn't need him. She's very kick-butt all on her own. But the knight is kind and cute and so she decides to let him tag along. At least for now.

I was so engrossed in my art that I didn't even hear the first knock on my door.

The second, of course, was louder. And, more annoyingly, followed by Mom entering my room without my permission. I would have objected more strongly to the parental invasion, except that she was carrying a tray of food. My growling stomach was ready and willing to be bribed into forgiveness.

I shoved the sketchbook under my math book and made like I was working out complex equations. Skipping dinner for homework was acceptable. Skipping dinner to draw was most certainly not.

"Lots of homework?" Mom asked in her best sympathetic voice as she set the tray on my desk. Mmm, lasagna. "Or are we just doing the avoiding-your-family thing again?"

Sigh. No such thing as a guilt-free meal delivery. "Um, a little of each?"

Mom didn't look all that amused. "I see," she said. "So how was school?"

"It was totally awesome!" I cried with cheerleader level enthusiasm. "I suddenly love it there! I hope that I can stay forever and ever and ever."

Mom frowned. "Don't be cute, Maddy. I'm serious."

She wanted serious? Should I tell her about my onstage

humiliation? She'd probably figure out a way to blame me for it.

"If you must know, I'm still not a big fan of the place."

She gave me her pitying look. "I'm sorry, sweetie. Do you want to talk about it?"

I scowled. "Not unless you've suddenly come up with a plan that lets me return to my old school," I shot back. "Otherwise, I've got a lot of homework and should really get to it."

"Fine," Mom replied, standing up quickly, trying to mask her hurt, but failing miserably. "Enjoy your dinner. Yell if you'd like dessert. Grandma made a terrific banana cream pie. I can have Emily bring you up a slice so you won't have to deal with my nosing into your business again."

Stabbed through the heart with a guilt-coated dagger. Damn, she was good.

"Sorry, Mom," I apologized. "It's just . . . well, it's complicated."

She sighed. "I know, sweetie," she said. "Moving's been rough on all of us."

"Except Emily."

"She's eight. It's easy to make new friends when you're eight," Mom said, sounding a bit wistful. I suddenly wondered if she'd made any new friends herself since we moved and she started her new job.

"Can't we just move back to Boston?" I blurted out before I could stop myself. "It'd be so much better for all of us."

Mom's face regained its pained look. "You know we don't

have the money, Maddy," she reminded me. "I've been working two jobs and—"

"Right. Never mind," I replied quickly. Maybe too quickly. "Anyway, I've got to work. I'll catch up with you later, okay?"

Mom opened her mouth, as if to say something, then seemed to change her mind and closed it again. "Okay," she said. "Hope you're able to get it all done. Let me know if you need any help." She headed out of my room, shutting the door behind her.

Once she was gone, I reached under my math book and pulled out the sketch I'd been working on, studying it with a critical eye. I was psyched with how cool it was coming out. Too bad I'd have to wait to finish it tomorrow. I stuffed it back into my math book. I hadn't been lying when I told Mom I had a lot of homework. And if I didn't start now, I wouldn't get to play Fields of Fantasy later. And that meant I wouldn't get to meet up with Sir Leo, which, let's face it, was sure to be the highlight of my miserable day. The one person who didn't think I was a total loser freak.

So I studied and studied and studied some more. Until my eyes grew bleary and I could barely read the equations on the page, never mind have the mental capacity to solve them. Finally deciding to call it a night, I shut my book and wheeled myself over to my computer desk, switching on the machine and crossing my fingers Sir Leo would be online. It was later than I realized—and I prayed that he hadn't gone to bed yet.

Bing!

Evidently not. The second I logged in, he pinged me. Butterflies in my stomach fluttered their approval. Gah. What was it about him that made me all crazy? I'd never even met the guy! And yet every time we met, I got all goofy and girly inside.

[SirLeo] M'lady! You have arrived. I have been going mad without thee.

[Allora] I hadn't realized thou would even notice my absence!

[SirLeo] But of course! I depend on you to do all the damage with your mighty fire spells.

[Allora] (Ohhh, I see how it is. I knew you kept me around for something.)

[SirLeo] In fact, I had been ready to send out a search party for thee. Worried, perhaps, you had run afoul of a deadly swine.

[Allora] LOL.

[SirLeo] Or kidnapped by mad goblins.

[Allora] He-he.

[SirLeo] Or ravished by leprechauns, even, desperate for their lucky charms.

[Allora] . . .

[SirLeo] Or, um, I don't know . . . Something else really terrible and bad. :-P

[Allora] (I was nearly vanquished by evil mathematics, if you must know.)

[SirLeo] (Ah, the dreaded homework hound. The most foul beast of all.)

[Allora] (No kidding.)

[SirLeo] (I've had a ton lately, myself. Stupid pop quiz today, too. Bleh.)

[Allora] (Ugh. Don't even get me started. It's like teachers think we have nothing better to do with our lives than to come home and do more schoolwork.)

[SirLeo] (It's coz they're old and have no lives and want to punish those who do.)

[Allora] (LOL. That must be it.)

[SirLeo] (So how was your day? I mean, besides the homework.)

[Allora] (Not the greatest, to tell you the truth.)

[SirLeo] (☹ I'm sorry. If it makes you feel better, mine wasn't any better.)

[Allora] (Awhhh. What happened?)

[SirLeo] (Well, it's just that there's this . . . Bleh. It's too long a story to type out.)

[Allora] . . .

[SirLeo] (Let's just say I have really lame friends.)

[Allora] (Why? What did they do?)

[SirLeo] (They just think they're soooo cool, you know? And I think they get off on ruining people's lives.)

[Allora] (Ah. I know a few people like that myself.)

A certain Billy Henderson and the Haters came to mind. But I tried to focus on what Ms. Reilly had said. That it wasn't enough to make them *think* their bullying didn't bother me. I had to get to a point where it really didn't. And focusing on it wouldn't get me there.

[SirLeo] (Honestly, sometimes I really think I'd be better off without friends.)

[Allora] (Heh. You don't mean that. Trust me.)

[SirLeo] (Ummm . . . You haven't met my friends.)

I drummed my fingers on the desk, a bit annoyed. Yeah, right. He could say that because he had no idea how that actually felt. How lonely and depressing it was to have absolutely no one at your school to talk to. To eat lunch with. To share stories about stupid teachers with. Even sucky friends would be better than no friends at all, in my opinion.

[Allora] (What's so bad about these friends of yours?)

[SirLeo] (Um, IDK. It's just . . . well, you know how they say, "If your friends jumped off a cliff, would you?")

[Allora] (LOL, ya.)

[SirLeo] (Sometimes I think I would.)

[Allora] (No way. I can't see it.)

[SirLeo] (Heh. This is why I like talking to you. You have no idea what I'm like IRL.)

[Allora] (IRL?)

[SirLeo] (In real life.)

[Allora] (Are you that diff?)

[SirLeo] (Well, no. I mean, I don't know. It's just . . . I feel like I can be myself around you. Not always feeling like I'm acting. Worried what people think about me.)

[Allora] (Ah, I see.)

[SirLeo] (It's, like, everyone thinks I'm this other guy, you know? And I can never be myself 'cause they would think I'm a total freak.)

[Allora] ; ;

Strange, I thought as I typed in the Japanese emoticon for tears. He seemed so confident. So cool. Was that only because his role of knight in shining armor in the game allowed him to act that way? Was he completely different in real life? I guess it wasn't that shocking. After all, he probably had the totally wrong idea about me as well. Probably thought I was cool and popular and beautiful. . . .

I turned back to the conversation.

[Allora] (Give me an example.)

[SirLeo] (An example?)

[Allora] (You know, like, when you're forced to act unlike yourself.)

[SirLeo] (Oh . . . um, IDK.)

[Allora] . . .

[SirLeo] (kk. Like, I can't tell people I'm into . . . certain things.)

[Allora] (Certain things? Like what?)

Sir Leo shrugs.

[Allora] (Come on! Michael Jackson CDs? Do you have a leg warmer fetish?)

[SirLeo] (LOL!! No!)

[Allora] (So what is this horrible, terrible, crazy thing that you like that you won't even tell your BFFs?)

[SirLeo] (Whoa, you're sooo pushy today.)

[Allora] (He-he. Yup, yup.)

Allora pushes Sir Leo playfully.

[SirLeo] (LOL. kk, fine. But now you're going to think I'm a total geek, too.)

[Allora] (Hmm. . . . Well, I guess it's just a risk you're going to have to take.)

[SirLeo] (Fine. I like . . . comic books.)

Allora raises an eyebrow.

Sir Leo blushes.

[Allora] (Comic books? Your deep dark secret is . . . comic books?)

[Sir Leo] (Um, yeah. Stupid, huh?)

[Allora] (No bodies buried in the basement? No undying crush on Rosie O'Donnell?)

[SirLeo] (Just comic books. But I'm really into them. I mean, obsessively so.)

[Allora] (How obsessive is obsessively so? I mean, do you go to comic-cons? Have you seen *300* more than 300 times? Do you have Superman, volume one?)

[SirLeo] (LOL. Yes, maybe, and I wish. In that order, sadly.)

[Allora] (So you're a geek.)

[SirLeo] (Er, I guess?)

I suddenly realized I was grinning from ear to ear. He was a geek. A real geek. Just like me. How cool was that?

[Allora] (Do you like manga or just American comics?)

[SirLeo] (Um, American. Marvel stuff, mostly. I don't really know too much about manga. Why? Do you like it?)

[Allora] (Oh, yeah, I love it. You should definitely give it a try.)

[SirLeo] (kk. Maybe I will.)

[Allora] (There are a lot of great ones out there. I can recommend some if you want.)

[SirLeo] (Yeah? That'd be cool.)

[Allora] (No problem. I'll draw you up a list for next time we play.)

[SirLeo] (So, um, you don't think I'm totally lame then?)

[Allora] (Are you kidding? I think it's way cool.)

[SirLeo] (Hmm. Though I haven't told you about my Spider-Man Underoos collection . . .)

Allora stares.

[SirLeo] (Just kidding.)

[Allora] (Phew.)

[SirLeo] (They, uh, don't make my size.)

[Allora] (He-he.)

[SirLeo] (He-he.)

He-he indeed. He was so funny and sweet. How could he possibly believe that people wouldn't like him for who he really was? Then again, no one liked me for who I was, so maybe he was onto something there. Still, it seemed a terrible way to live your life. To be forced to hide this fascinating, funny, cool person who had a real passion for something special and instead go around acting like a no-personality sheep, just to keep your friends list intact. Skipping comic-cons to go to football games. Sneaking comics under *Sports Illustrated*. It was sad, really.

[Allora] (I bet your friends don't know you play video games, either.)

[SirLeo] (Um, yeah. No way.)

[Allora] (And if you told them, they'd make fun of you and call you a loser?)

[SirLeo] (Basically.)

[Allora] (Wow. Cool friends. Wish I had me some of those.)

[SirLeo] (Yeah, well, it's not that easy. Once you're in a crowd . . .)

[Allora] (But what's the sense of having friends who don't respect who you really are? Real friends, even if they don't like the things you do, still respect the fact that you do them.)

[SirLeo] (Sigh. I know, you're right.)

[Allora] (Of course. I'm always right, remember?)

[SirLeo] (LOL. You know, I'm really glad I met you, Allora. You're not like any of my real life friends. You're special.)

Allora blushes.

[Allora] (Yeah. Special needs, right?)

Sir Leo laughs.

[SirLeo] (Hey—I'm trying to compliment you.)

[Allora] (I know. I'm just teasing.)

No response for a moment, then . . .

[SirLeo] (Argh. I can't take it! I wish you lived in Farming-dale. I'd totally ask you out.)

My heart jumped to my throat as I stared at his words. Farm-ingdale? Okay, there probably were a ton of Farmingdales out there, right? He didn't necessarily mean Farmingdale, New Hampshire, the town I was currently living in, right?

But what if he did? Mercy, what if he actually went to my school? What if Sir Leo was someone I knew in real life? Like, what if we passed each other in the halls every day and never knew it? That would be crazy!

And really, really cool.

My mind launched into full-on fantasy mode. Sir Leo asking me out on a date. Meeting him in person for the first time. Laughing and sharing and not relying on a keyboard to bare our souls. Wandering the real world, instead of the game, holding hands and talking for hours. The sun would set and he'd take me in his arms and kiss me like I'd never been kissed before.

I shook my head. *Stop it, Maddy,* I rebuked myself. There was no need to indulge in this kind of senseless fantasy. We could never take our friendship to the real-life level, even if we did happen to live in the same town. Because neither of us was the same person when the computer shut down and there was no way someone as cool as he would want to go out with someone like me. A freak girl. The laughingstock of the high school.

Better to keep it all online.

[SirLeo] (Great. Now I've scared you off again. I'm sorry.)

[Allora] (No, sorry. It's just . . . I don't know . . .)

[SirLeo] (Not a good idea. Right. I know. I'm just . . . well, it's so limiting to type online. I want to tell you all this stuff and I just . . . never mind. It was stupid. Forget it.)

My heart felt like it was tearing in two as I read his pain typed across my screen. He really did like me. But which "me" was that? The online beautiful elf me, that's which. The one who sounded brave and independent and didn't care what people thought of her. My real-life self would truly disappoint.

[Allora] (I'm sorry. It's just . . . I think it's better this way. But I still want to play, okay? As much as possible. You're, like, turning into this great friend.)

Sir Leo grins.

[SirLeo] (You're a great friend, too. I had been thinking of quitting the game altogether till you came along. Now I'm rushing home from school just to meet up with you to play.)

My celebratory butterflies launched into another parade. Even though we'd never move beyond this online friendship, relationship, whatever you wanted to call it, we'd always have Fields of Fantasy. And maybe that was enough.

[SirLeo] (Anyway, let's play, okay? All this heavy talk . . . I think I need to be mindless for a bit.)

[Allora] (kk. Let's go do that Archmage Vernon quest. I am

in total need of more Upper City rep so I can get keyed for
Carathon. Oh, and I want to farm some Bird People, too,
if we have time—see if we can get any air elementals to
sell at the AH. Need to start saving my gold for my mount.
Though I have been eyeing that BoE Staff of the Night Owl.
IDK if I want to just buy it or see if we can get it to drop off
the boss in HeavensGate. I thotbotted it and it looks like
it's a pretty rare drop. . . .)

[SirLeo] (LOL. kk. Funny. You'd never know you were a
complete noob just a short time ago! Now you're a total
gamer girl, huh?)

Allora grins.

[Allora] (Someone taught me well.)

[SirLeo] Well, then that noble someone should be re-
warded. Greatly. Showered with much gold, I should think.

Allora shoves Sir Leo playfully.

[Allora] (Yeah, right. You wish.)

Sir Leo laughs.

[SirLeo] (Fine, fine. No respect. I see. Go ahead and be that
way.)

[Allora] (Thanks! I will.)

Sir Leo sighs deeply.

[SirLeo] So, my fair maiden, where wouldst thou like to
adventure today?

We slipped back into characters, forgetting the real world
once again. Together we worked on quests, won treasure,
gained skills, then finally settled down on the top of a cliff

not far from the Elf Tree Café, overlooking a cascading waterfall. The game crickets chirped happily as Sir Leo and Allora sat side by side, gazing at the virtual sunset, a rich, fiery display that only a high-end graphics card could offer.

Sir Leo cuddled closer to Allora, putting his arm around her shoulder.

[SirLeo] It's so beautiful here. So peaceful.

[Allora] No monsters to spoil it.

[SirLeo] (Or homework, or friends, or any real-life crap.)

[Allora] (Too true.)

[SirLeo] You are truly beautiful, m'lady. I am very lucky to have met you.

[Allora] And I, you. For I would have been still battling those wolves.

Sir Leo laughs.

[SirLeo] Well, I am honored to have been of some sort of service. But you have paid me back tenfold already.

Allora smiles.

Sir Leo kisses Allora tenderly.

I stared at the screen, heart drumming against my chest a million miles a minute. He kissed me. He just actually kissed me. Okay, so it was really Sir Leo kissing Allora. But still!

Crazy how a video game could get my pulse racing. What to do, what to do?

There really was only one thing.

Allora kisses Sir Leo back.
Sir Leo sighs contently.

I let out my own real-life contented sigh. It was clear that our characters were falling for each other. And I had to admit Allora's feelings for Sir Leo weren't so far from the ones I felt for the boy who played him. Whoever he was. Wherever he lived.

If only it *were* possible for us to meet. Would it be awkward? Would we both be shy? Or would the connection we'd made over the game hold and cause us to instantly fall in love? Was he cute? Would he think I was pretty? Was he a good kisser? Did he like to cuddle in real life?

We said our good nights and I reluctantly logged out of the game, then headed over to my bed. I curled up under the covers, hugging my stuffed bear against my chest. I tried to tell myself for the millionth time that this was enough. That my virtual relationship was very fulfilling and was all I really needed. That there was no reason to want to meet Sir Leo in real life, even if he did, by some freaky random chance, live in the same town as me and go to the same school.

But unfortunately my heart wasn't buying it. Because I was in love with Sir Leo.

Ms. REILLY was as good as her word. By Friday, she'd gotten all the necessary forms signed to start the first ever manga club at Hannah Dustin High School. I'd finished the flyers and, as soon as I got the go-ahead from her, started posting them around school. They had come out looking really cool, though at the last minute I decided against using my own artwork. Didn't want to offer up free ammunition for the Haters to use to make fun of me with. Instead, I found some cool clip art from the *Sojo Beat* website and decorated using that instead. We scheduled the first meeting for Wednesday, to be held in the school library. Up until the last moment I still wasn't convinced anyone would show up. Even if Sarah was right about there being other manga fans at school, that didn't mean they'd necessarily jump at the idea of joining a club to talk about it. Especially a club run by Freak Girl.

Still, it was probably worth a try. Because if it did work, if people did come, it'd be great. I'd finally meet kids in this stupid school that cared about something besides the latest sale at the mall. We'd all become friends and start hanging out. People would actually say hi in the halls and I'd have friends to eat with at lunch.

This really was a great idea. I'm so glad I suggested it to Ms. Reilly.

"Whatcha doin', Freak Girl?"

Oh, great. Billy. Just the person to put a damper on my day. I finished pressing the flyer against the wall, making sure it was properly stuck before turning around to deal with my dearest BFF. He stood behind me, arms crossed, wearing a Bruins jersey and a big scowl on his face, glaring at me expectantly. At least he was without his little posse for once.

I considered walking away. But something inside of me stirred, stopping me in my tracks. Some sort of weird sense of self-respect, long buried. I remembered Ms. Reilly's words. *You've got to get to the point where it really doesn't bother you. You gotta stop giving them your power.* I'd made a vow. I was following Ms. Reilly's advice from now on. And I wasn't going to let him bother me anymore.

"What does it look like, brainiac?" I shot back, even surprising myself with the force of my jab. "I'll give you three guesses. No, wait. Don't strain yourself. Wouldn't want to hurt your head." I waved a flyer in his face, channeling my inner mean girl. "See these? I'm hanging them . . . on a . . . wall!" I spoke the last part slowly, as if addressing a dim-witted child. Which wasn't far off the mark, now that I thought about it. "With tape," I added, waving the dispenser. "You know—sticky, sticky!"

A thrill tickled my stomach as Billy took a step back, a confused look on his formerly arrogant face. He certainly hadn't expected that reaction from me.

Woot! Score one for Maddy!

"Uh, yeah. Got that," Billy retorted. He ripped down the flyer I'd just put up and studied it with narrowed eyes. "But what on earth is a manga club?" he asked, pronouncing it "mahn-jah." "Does that mean 'vampire' in Swahili or something?"

"Funny, no. It doesn't. But I wouldn't expect your pea brain to know any Japanese, so don't feel too bad." I was impressing myself with my witty comebacks. Who knew I had it in me?

"Ooh, you're so smart, Freak Girl. I wish I could be a nerd like you and start a mahn-jah club at school."

"It's manga," I corrected. "Hard 'g.'"

"Whatever," he said, though I noticed his face had grown kind of red.

I rolled my eyes and moved down the hall, looking for the next place to hang a flyer. This was the guy who practically the whole school worshipped? Suddenly he seemed like nothing more than a pathetic little twerp. He followed me, standing way too close for comfort as I affixed tape to the paper. Obviously trying to unnerve me.

Don't let him bother you, I reminded myself. *Don't let him win.*

"You still haven't told me what manga is," he reminded me, leaning against a locker.

"Learn to Google," I replied. "Wikipedia is your friend."

Billy looked down at the flyer. "Oh, it's lame-o comic books, isn't it?"

"Brilliant deduction." I clapped my hands for him. "Though manga is a Japanese art form. So it's not like we're covering Superman or anything." I didn't know why I was bothering to explain, really.

"Wow, Freak Girl. That sounds way cool." Billy crumpled up the flyer and tossed it, quarterback style, down the hall. I kept my face blank, forcing myself to stay calm. I pulled out another flyer from my bag and hung it up a few feet away. Good thing I'd made plenty of copies.

Billy followed me, still scowling. Probably pissed he hadn't been able to make me cry yet. Hope he wasn't holding his breath waiting, because it was so not going to happen.

"So who do you expect to join your little geeky comic book club?" he demanded. "Last I checked we don't have many *Japanese* students here at Hannah Dustin."

I almost burst out laughing. He couldn't be that stupid, could he? "Do you live under a total rock?" I asked incredulously. "Have you ever been to a bookstore? A library? Manga's huge. Tons of American kids read it."

Billy's face darkened. Evidently I'd struck a nerve. "I don't . . . waste my time in bookstores," he retorted. "Libraries are for chumps."

"Right." I gave him my sweetest smile. "It's okay, Billy, really."

"Shut up, Freak Girl."

"I know you're only trying to hurt me because you feel very angry inside."

Billy stared at me like I had three heads and a carrot for a nose. "What?" he cried, his face red with rage. "What are you talking about?"

Wow. He was just as easy to get a rise out of as the people he abused each day. I chuckled at the irony.

"Why are you laughing? Huh, Freak Girl?" he demanded, totally losing his cool at this point. "You're stupid. You're a freak. No one likes you. They all think you're a loser."

I shot him an unconcerned smile and walked farther down the hall. He didn't follow me this time. Out of the corner of my eye I say him rip down my flyer, throw it to the ground, and stomp on it with his foot.

"Wow," remarked a pretty blond upperclassman who stood nearby, watching his temper tantrum. "Looks like Billy has some anger issues to work out."

I laughed. "Totally," I said, my insides warming. "He can be such a freak boy."

WEDNESDAY TOOK forever to come and then the school day dragged on endlessly. I could barely pay attention to my teachers as my mind raced in nervous anticipation. Would anyone show up? Would they be cool? Would they want to be friends with me? I tried to tell myself that it didn't matter. That I'd be fine either way. But my heart wasn't buying it this time. I wanted this to be a success. Badly. To show the Haters. To show everyone.

After what seemed an eternity, the last-period bell finally rang and everyone jumped from their seats, eager to abandon the building or start whatever after-school activity they had planned for that afternoon. I didn't even give my usual early bus a second glance as I headed straight to the library, psyched there was finally an extracurricular I could pad my college application with that wouldn't have me cringing with boredom and pain.

When I got there, I saw that Ms. Reilly had already arrived and was in the process of positioning a cart that held a TV/DVD combo along with three precariously balanced pizza boxes in front of a large circular table with lots of chairs.

I raised an eyebrow. "Three pizzas?" I queried. "Seems a bit optimistic, don't you think? I mean, we don't even know if anyone will show up to this thing."

Ms. Reilly laughed and set the pizza boxes on the wood table. "You worry too much, Maddy," she scolded. "And besides, what's the worst that can happen? We'd have to eat all the pizza by ourselves? What a tragedy."

"True," I said, opening the box and helping myself to a hot slice. The cheese burned the roof of my mouth and I quickly set it down on a paper plate. "What books did you get?"

"I thought we'd start with a little *Fullmetal Alchemist*," she said, reaching into a cardboard box and setting a stack of manga on the table. "And maybe, if there's time, we could watch some anime. I brought in *.hack//SIGN*. Have you heard of it? It's based on a video game—sort of like Fields of Fantasy."

"Nice," I said, impressed by her selections. And here I had been worried she'd whip out a *Pokémon* or *Sailor Moon* in a lame, misguided adult effort to be cool. But Ms. Reilly, she was the real deal.

"Someday," she added, her eyes shining, "I'll make you all watch something real old-school. Like the anime they had on TV when I was growing up."

I grinned wickedly. "Huh. I didn't realize they had TV back then."

She balled up a piece of paper and threw it at me. "Watch it, missie," she warned.

"Just kidding."

She grabbed a slice of pizza and set it on a plate. "I'm not exactly a grandma. We even had Internet when I was a kid, I'll have you know."

"Internet. I'll give you that. But not YouTube or MySpace."

She shook her head. "Yes, yes," she admitted. "It's true. As a child I was severely deprived of the opportunity to post my personal information online for all the world's nut jobs to see. In fact, I even used a diary made of paper instead of a blog. Sad, really, now that I think about it."

I grinned. "Yeah, yeah. So what's the old-school anime you were talking about?"

"Have you ever heard of *Voltron*?"

I shook my head.

She thought for a moment. "I guess I'd describe it as kind of an anime *Transformers*. These five kids had spaceships that they combined into one giant robot . . ."

"Right. I see. Sounds . . . um, cool." Not really, but I was willing to do the retro thing if she was all into it.

Ms. Reilly laughed. "I'll teach you kids to appreciate the classics if it's the last thing I do."

"You are too cool for school, Ms. Reilly." I bit into my pizza and scanned the room. Everything was set up. Now we just needed bodies.

"Um, is this, like, the manga club?"

I looked up to see a gangly, mousy brunette—all legs and arms—with pigtails and braces hovering at the library door. A freshman from the look of it, dressed in an adorable plaid pleated skirt, leg warmers, and a vintage-looking Hello Kitty top. On closer examination I realized she had tiny cat ears bobby pinned to her headband.

"Yes, you're definitely in the right place," I said, throwing my potential new BFF a smile. She grinned back and pranced over to the table, grabbing a slice of pizza and stuffing it in her mouth.

"Nice," she said, her mouth filled with gooey cheese. "I couldn't believe it when I saw the flyer. Like, how cool is it to have a manga club right here at school? I mean, sure I belong to a billion online manga clubs. You know, like, where you have forums and everything? Cosplay.com for example. Great site. But then, of course, like, online you end up knowing people, but you don't really know them. I mean, you do in a way, but it's not the same as knowing them in real life. Um, not that I consider online life not real, ha-ha, but you know what I mean, right?"

She paused to take a much-needed breath. I waved.

"I'm Maddy," I said, while I had a chance to get a word in edgewise.

She wiggled her fingers, with nails pink and chipped. "I'm Jessica. You can call me Jessie," she replied. "Thanks for starting this club."

"No problem." I liked her already.

Three more kids filtered in. A stocky sophomore named

Ed that I recognized from art class. A Goth girl, Treena—call me Black Raven—Jones, who informed everyone she preferred vampire manga and had several volumes of TOKYOPOP's *Chibi Vampire* on hand to prove it. Rounding out the crew was a total emo boy who introduced himself as David. He dressed all in black and was desperately trying to look mopey and miserable. Problem was he was obviously so excited about the club he kept grinning widely, which seriously detracted from the life-stinks-and-then-you-die look he was going for.

I couldn't believe it. Where had these kids been hiding the past few months? How had I missed them in the halls? Had they, too, been quietly slipping through the school day, trying to blend in and not be noticed so they wouldn't risk becoming the kind of target I had become to the Haters? These were my peeps, coming out of the woodwork, ready to get their inner geek on.

This was better than I'd even imagined.

Sarah the *Shojo Beat* girl from the other day showed up a few minutes later, followed by Matt and Luke, who immediately informed us they felt American graphic novels should be part of the club, too. Everyone sat down and I realized the table was nearly full. The pizza was not going to go to waste after all.

"I'm Maddy," I introduced myself when everyone had seated and grabbed a slice. "Ms. Reilly asked me to serve as your club president—at least until we get off the ground and can hold elections."

"Sounds good to me," Black Raven asserted. "Thanks for starting the group."

"Yeah, thanks," the others chimed in. "This rocks."

I beamed. "No problem," I said. "Shall we get started?"

We'd all settled in at the table, everyone chatting with one another as we stuffed our faces full of pizza. We talked about manga, graphic novels, anime, and even life in general. David told us about a poetry book he was writing and Jessie showed us her extensive collection of Final Fantasy figurines she'd gotten off eBay. Black Raven explained the mythology of vampires in modern myths and Ed pulled out some drawings he'd done of Train from the *Black Cat* series.

I got so lost in the conversations that at first I didn't notice the solitary figure leaning against the library doorjamb, watching us from a distance. That was until Black Raven pointed him out with a chunky silver-ringed finger. "Oh, my God. What's *he* doing here?" she stage-whispered to the group.

Everyone turned to stare at the intruder. My eyes widened as I realized it was none other than Chad Murray himself. Spying on the manga club just as I'd been spying on drama practice last week. My heart skipped a beat as I accidentally caught his eye. He gave me a half smile. I quickly dropped my gaze, staring down at my pizza plate instead, reminding myself that I should stay away from him. He was one of the Haters. He was the enemy.

"Intruder alert, intruder alert," Black Raven warned in a fake robot voice. "We have been spotted. I repeat, Operation

Manga has been infiltrated by the StuckUp Syndicate. We may need backup, people. They're armed with hair gel and I don't think they're afraid to use it."

The others burst into laughter. I stifled a giggle, then felt bad when I peeked back over and saw his face. If I didn't know better, I'd say he looked . . . hurt. But that was impossible. Why would someone like him, one of the most popular kids in school, care what a few comic book geeks thought of him?

"Now, Treena," Ms. Reilly rebuked, though I could tell she was trying not to laugh, "this is an open club. Anyone who wants to join is allowed to." She waved over to Chad. "Come sit down with us if you'd like," she told him. "There's plenty of room."

Chad took a step forward, then retreated, a conflicted look on his face. What was up with him? Did he really want to join our manga club? Had hell frozen over? Had pigs learned to fly? I mean, not that I'd mind if he wanted to join. But it just seemed . . . weird . . . that he would.

"Ms. Reilly, let's be realistic," Matt said, turning to the teacher. "Chad Murray is *not* exactly our peeps."

"Yeah. No way someone like him would want to join our club," chimed in Jessie. "More likely he's on some special re-con mission for Billy the Butthead. Getting the four-one-one on how we operate so they can figure out new ways to torture and make our lives miserable."

"Stupid brainless sheep," David muttered. He waved at Chad then made a face. "Go home and listen to your Justin Timberlake CD!" he yelled. The club collapsed into giggles and then went back into their cosplay conventions discussion.

I stole another glance over at the library entrance, watching as Chad started to slink away. I looked back at the table. A lively debate had begun about sewing your own costume versus buying one on eBay and they'd all but forgotten the intruder. Seeing my opening, I jumped up from my seat and headed over. At the very least I could find out what he wanted. Apologize for the others' bad behavior, maybe.

"Chad," I called out to him as I reached the hall. He stopped and turned around.

"Hey," he said, stuffing his hands in his pockets. He was wearing a blue hoodie and slouchy jeans. Of course, he could be wearing nothing but a trash bag and still look like the hottest thing on Earth.

I shifted from foot to foot, feeling suddenly shy. Why had I come out here to talk to him again? And what was I supposed to say now that I had his attention? His sky-blue eyes had turned my brain into mush, as usual. Argh.

"Don't mind them," I said, finally, gesturing into the library. "They were just . . ."

Getting back at you for all the things you and your friends did to them? Bullying the bullies? Scoring points for the losing team?

"Just teasing," I finished lamely, losing all my nerve.

Chad scuffed the toe of his sneaker against the cement

hall floor. "Whatever," he muttered. "I'm sure I deserved it in some way or another." He looked up at me. "How's it going in there, anyway? Looks like you had a good turnout."

I beamed, unable to help myself. "Yeah, it's awesome. A lot of people showed up. I was really surprised."

"I saw your posters around school," he continued. "And I figured I'd come see what it was all about. Is it like an art club or something? Do you guys draw comics?"

"Oh, no. We just read manga and watch anime," I replied. "Though, I mean, we could draw, I suppose. I hadn't thought of that. I wonder if people would be interested."

He grinned suddenly. "You could teach them."

"Teach them?" I cocked my head in confusion.

"How to draw like you do."

I blushed furiously. "Oh, I'm not that good," I stammered. "I don't think anyone would want to learn from me."

"You never know," he said with a shrug. "And you are, too, that good. I saw your drawing, remember? Stop being so modest."

I couldn't believe he was complimenting me again. What did that mean? Was there any chance in the universe that he actually liked me? That he might be flirting?

"So did you, um, want to join us?" I asked. The second the question left my lips, I regretted it. Of course the school hottie did not want to join our little motley crew of manga lovers. He had a thousand better things to do with people who were a thousand times more rich and good-looking.

Then again, he just said he came to check us out. So maybe . . .

"Well, I—"

Chad barely got the two words out before Chelsea came prancing around the corner. "Chad, what are you *doing*?" the resident princess demanded. She tossed her long locks over her shoulder, then planted her hands on her narrow hips. She was dressed in a pair of fitted Seven jeans and a pink cashmere sweater. The look screamed classy, beautiful, and rich and I felt like a total schlub standing next to her in my skull-patterned baby doll dress.

Chad winced, as if he'd been caught doing something incredibly wrong. I guess he had been, in a way. Fraternizing with the enemy and all that. I wondered what he was about to say before she showed up. Guess now I'd never know.

"Slumming it, I see," she added, giving me her infamous princess look of utter disdain. I so wanted to punch her in the face, but I reminded myself of what Ms. Reilly said about letting them get to me. Chelsea wasn't worth it.

"Shut up, Chelsea," Chad muttered under his breath, so low she probably couldn't hear him. Still, he *had* said it. Out loud. Hmm. Was there some dissension in the Hater ranks these days?

"What did you say?" she demanded.

"I said we were just talking," Chad mumbled, his face turning a ripe tomato color.

"Well, finish up, please," Chelsea ordered. "Now. Billy sent me to find you. He said you turned off your cell phone."

She stared at him, accusingly, as if he'd been caught killing puppy dogs.

"Maybe I didn't want to be disturbed."

"Oh, yeah, sure." She laughed, as if what he was saying was totally ridiculous. "Anyway, we're all going out to Friendly's for dinner. Everyone who's anyone is going to be there." She threw a pointed look at me, as if she felt the need to further emphasize that I wasn't invited and therefore wasn't anybody. "You *have* to come."

"I don't know," Chad hedged, raking a hand through his blond hair in a way that nearly left me a soppy puddle on the floor. "I'm really beat."

Chelsea laughed—a squeaky chuckle that sounded annoyingly like tinkling Christmas bells. "Oh, Chad, you're so funny," she said, giggling. "For a moment, I actually believed you." She grabbed him by his hood and started dragging him down the hall. "Come on, silly," she said, still tugging. "Let's go already."

Chad allowed himself be dragged, but kept his eyes on me. Just before I turned to walk away, I saw him mouth the word "Sorry."

I shrugged, trying not to let the rising disappointment get to me. What did it matter, anyway? It wasn't like I had some burning desire for Chad Murray to join the manga club. He wouldn't fit in and everyone would feel awkward with him sitting there. It was for the best, really.

I headed back to the library, sitting down at my seat. Everyone turned to look at me, expectant looks on their faces.

"Sorry," I said, not wanting to explain. "I'm back."

"So, Maddy," Ms. Reilly addressed me, "I was just telling everyone how well you draw and now they all want to see some of your work."

I looked across the table. Sure enough, six eager faces peered back at me. Feeling self-conscious, I reached into my bag and pulled out my portfolio.

"I'm creating a new manga," I explained, pulling out a few sketches and laying them down on the table. "So I can enter this contest."

"What's it about?"

I explained about Allora getting sucked in to the computer and questing with her handsome hero to find a way back home. "Once she's home, she retains all of her character's powers," I added. "And she's able to brow beat all the bullies that used to pick on her, and able to turn the school cliques upside down. She goes from a freak girl . . ."—I held out drawing number one—"to a gamer girl." I held up the still unfinished final drawing of Allora. "Which is what I'm calling the book. As you can see, it's not quite done yet."

"Wow, that's so cool," remarked Ed, picking up one of the drawings. "You're really good."

"Totally," agreed David. "I love this one with her beating up on Willie, here. Hmm, I wonder who you based him on."

I grinned sheepishly. Everyone laughed.

"You should make him a little fatter," suggested Luke.

"And a lot uglier," added Sarah.

"Maddy, these are so awesome!" Jessie blurted out, flipping through the sketches. "It's so great you can draw. I can't draw to save myself. I love to read manga but I think it'd be the absolute coolest thing ever to draw it. Not that I'll ever be able to. But you can! How cool is that?"

The others laughed at her rambling, but not in a mean-spirited way. Soon she was giggling along with them.

"Well, maybe next week Maddy can give us a little demo," Ms. Reilly suggested. "Teach us all the basics."

A chorus of enthusiasm followed her suggestion. I smiled. How fun would that be? To teach others the art I loved so much. Finally have people appreciate me for what I could do.

Ms. Reilly announced it was time to watch the movie and pressed Play on the DVD player. For the rest of the session we watched *.hack//SIGN*, which really did remind me of Fields of Fantasy quite a bit. When it was over, we got up and headed to the exit together, still bantering over the finer points of the episode as we walked down the halls and out the front doors of the school, vowing to meet up again next week.

I got on the late bus and sat down in the back, feeling warm and fuzzy inside. I'd met new people who were cool and nice and didn't consider me a freak. And better still, I'd been able to share my passion with them and they actually understood why it was a big deal.

This was, without a doubt, the best school day yet.

WHAT'S WRONG with you?" my mother asked when I got home.

"Huh? What do you mean?"

"You're . . . you're . . . well, honey, you're smiling."

I laughed. "Ah. Sorry. I didn't realize I was. I can stop if it bothers you."

"Bothers me? Are you kidding? You have a beautiful smile. I just don't get to see it that often." Mom reached over and gave me a tight squeeze. I hugged her back.

"You're hugging? Since when do you two hug?" Emily asked, staring at us, hands on her hips.

I released Mom from the embrace. "Hey, Emily, want to show me your dance routines?"

The eight-year-old glared at me suspiciously. "You know, I saw a movie like this once," she determined. "Mom, I don't know how to tell you this, but I think Maddy has been taken over by pod people."

I rolled my eyes. "Come on, guys, it's not that weird, is it?" Had I really been such a miserable jerk all this time that one smile threw them for such a loop?

"Emily, where did you see a movie about pod people?" Mom demanded.

"Over at Dad's."

"Of course you did." Mom's happy face faded and she suddenly looked old. "Why did I even have to ask?"

"It was the 1994 remake, actually. Not the original," Emily provided helpfully.

"Yes, the R-rated one that's not appropriate for eight-year-olds. I figured as much."

Emily shrugged.

Mom turned and headed for the kitchen, shaking her head and muttering something about Dad's lack of ability to set appropriate boundaries for his children.

My upbeat mood dampened as I watched her go. "Nice one," I muttered to Emily, shaking my head.

"Whatever."

I held up my hands. "Fine," I said. "After all, I'm not the one always trying to get Mom and Dad back together."

"You honestly think Mom and Dad are going to get back together?" Emily rolled her blue eyes, having obviously faced reality finally. I didn't know whether to be relieved or sad.

"So you gonna watch my dance routine or what?" She looked up at me expectantly, her cupid bow mouth pursed as she waited for my answer.

I groaned. "As if you're really giving me a choice in the matter."

"Cool. Let's go outside." Emily dived to the hall closet in search of shoes. I glanced out the window.

"Um, it's raining," I noted. "Too bad. Guess you'll have to show me another time."

"What are you, the Wicked Witch of the West? Afraid you'll melt?"

"Right. Something like that. Without the green face paint."

"Oh, fine. You just don't want to see my routine." Emily pouted.

Sigh. "I asked to, didn't I?" I reminded her. "Let's just do it in the living room so I can watch from the couch."

Emily scrunched up her face. "Grandma doesn't want me to dance in there."

Of course she didn't. Not in the unicorn museum. I peered out the window. Rain was gushing down in torrents. "Well, I don't think Grandma's home," I told her. "Just be careful and I'm sure you'll be fine." I felt kind of guilty going against Grandma's rules, but at the same time I was so not in the mood to get soaked.

Emily thought it over for a moment, then nodded. "Okay," she said. "Let me go change into my costume."

"You don't have to . . ." I tried, but she was already gone. Sigh. Stupid me for bringing it up. Now I'd probably be stuck through an hour-and-a-half routine, complete with special effects and multiple costume changes. I reluctantly headed into the living room and plopped down on the couch. It was one of those antique Victorian ones that looked fancy but was totally uncomfortable to sit in. Meanwhile, our smooshy comfy couch and chairs sat gathering dust in a storage locker down the street.

Emily popped into the room a minute later, dressed in a tight half shirt and glitter miniskirt. She'd smeared turquoise eye shadow over her lids and a disturbing amount of blush on her cheeks, making her look like a crazy bag lady.

"Ta-da!" she cried, striking a pose.

"That's your costume?" I asked, raising an eyebrow.

"Umm, yeah," she said, her voice thick with scorn. "What did you expect, a tutu or something?"

"You're eight years old. It seems a reasonable assumption." She struck a pose, very Paris Hiltonesque. "Do you want to see me dance or not?"

I pulled my feet up and under me, waving a hand for her to go on. She dropped character to drag the coffee table to the side of the room and widen her dance space. Then she hit the power button on Grandma's antiquated stereo system (it even had a record player!) and spun the dial for maximum volume. A moment later my poor eardrums were bombarded with the sounds of Jessica Simpson.

My sister whirled around the room, like Britney Spears, jumping and twirling and dropping into splits. She was way into it, so unconscious of how bad she was and how silly she looked. I forced back my laughter.

"Brava!" I clapped as the first song ended. "Encore, encore!" Not that I especially wanted to sit through a second round, mind you, but it seemed the right thing to do.

Sure enough, she beamed at me, suddenly a little kid again. Gone was the jaded, world-weary girl she tried to portray on a daily basis. It was nice to see.

She reset the music and whirled around again, this time faster and more energetically—as if she were one of those whirling dervishes. She spun and she spun and I wondered how she didn't get dizzy and just—

Crash!

I cringed as Emily lost her balance and slammed right into Grandma's curio cabinet of porcelain monstrosities. The smashing of glass as the shelves came down was so loud it actually drowned out Jessica Simpson.

Not good. So not good.

"What is going on here?"

Even worse? Grandma just got home.

She entered the room, wearing a bright yellow raincoat, her watery blue eyes widening as she surveyed the destruction of all she held dear. Emily was in the process of trying to extract herself from the broken glass without cutting herself. Her face was red from dancing and tears were dripping down her cheeks.

In the background, Jessica crooned on about ditching some guy who may or may not have been Nick Lachey.

"My babies!" Grandma exclaimed, dropping to her knees and searching through the rubble for survivors. "My babies!"

Emily managed to stand up. "Sorry," she said. "I, um, slipped."

"What's going on here?" Mom burst into the room. She switched off the music and the room fell eerily silent.

"My babies!" Grandma repeated for the third time. I gritted my teeth. Yes, we got that already.

Emily retreated to the couch and snuggled up to me, as if trying to shield herself from the coming wrath. Good luck with that, kid.

"Mother, get up. I don't want you to cut yourself," Mom commanded. She helped Grandma to her feet and led her over to her rocking char. "I'll get your babies, don't worry."

Grandma allowed herself to be seated in the chair, fingering one of the glass horses she'd salvaged. "My babies," she muttered to herself.

Mom turned to us.

"Emily, you've been told you're not allowed to dance in the house," she scolded.

I waited for my sister to sell me out, but she surprisingly remained silent. I realized it was up to me to come clean.

"I told her to, Mom," I said. "It's my fault."

Mom released a long sigh, as if weary of the world. Maybe she was. She ran a hand through her hair and for the first time I realized she had some grays woven in with the brown.

"I think it's time you go upstairs to work on your homework," she said, sounding drained.

"I can help . . ." I tried, feeling really bad all of a sudden. Grandma looked so distraught. Emily was crying. Mom was furious.

And once again, it was all my fault. So much for best day ever.

"I think you've done enough," Mom replied in a tight voice. "I'll take care of this. Just go upstairs. You, too, Emily."

I took my sister's hand and led her out of the room and up the stairs. Crazy how I'd gone from being in a great mood to being miserable all over again. It just proved my point. We couldn't stay here much longer. It wasn't healthy for Emily. And it certainly wasn't good for me.

I sat Emily in front of the computer and let her surf the Disney website while I spread the drawings out on my desk and began to pencil in a new scene. I sketched Allora and Sir Leo, resting by the cascading waterfall, just as we had done the night before in real—make that virtual—life. But instead of being content in Allora's arms, Sir Leo looked worried.

"*So now what?*" he asked, turning to Allora. "*You've got the potion you need to go home. Will you take me with you?*"

Allora shook her head. "*You belong here in this fantasy world. You have no place on Earth. You'd hate it there.*"

Sir Leo looked crushed. "*I wouldn't hate it if you were there. I don't want to lose you. We could make it work between us. It doesn't have to stop here.*"

Allora sighed deeply. "*I don't know,*" she said. "*I'm not sure you would like me in real life. I'm a lot different there, you know. I don't even look the same."*

"I don't care if you look like an ugly troll with warts," Sir Leo declared, taking her hand in his. *"I love you."*

I set down my pen and sighed. Obviously real life was once again popping up in my manga. I guess it was good, in a way. It certainly gave a more emotional feel to the book. At the same time, it was no longer a blissful escape from my day-to-day problems.

I wistfully traced my finger along my drawing of Sir Leo. What was he like in real life? I was dying to know. Was it worth the risk meeting him? Knowing that a real-life encounter could end our online friendship forever?

I glanced over at the computer. Emily had evidently gotten bored and had climbed onto my bed and fallen asleep. Currently snoring like a trooper. Maybe I'd sign in to Fields of Fantasy to see if he was online. I missed him badly and wanted nothing more than to hang out with him and play the game. Lose myself in the virtual world for a few hours.

But sadly, my dashing knight in shining armor was nowhere to be found. A wave of disappointment washed over me. Where was he? What was he up to? Stuck doing homework? Eating a late dinner with his family? Or was he out and about, hanging with his friends . . . or worse, with another girl?

The idea made my stomach twist into a knot. I hadn't

really given much thought to the fact that Sir Leo could very well have a girlfriend. Sure, he never mentioned one, but then again, we didn't talk all that much about our personal lives. In fact, I had no reason to believe he wasn't totally dating some hot, popular chick in real life. A cheerleader, maybe. Or the student body president. Some blond airhead who didn't understand him at all. She didn't know his secret love for role-playing or comic books. She didn't know the sweet, sensitive soul, well hidden behind the mask he wore to school. She didn't know the real Sir Leo, the boy grappling with who he was and who he wanted to be.

And yet, she had him.

I thunked my head against my desktop, completely depressed. I tried to remind myself that I was projecting. That this hypothetical girlfriend likely didn't even exist. After all, Sir Leo had talked about meeting me in real life and he certainly didn't seem the type who would cheat on his girlfriend. More than likely he was single. For now. Who knew? He could, right at this very moment, be sharing a first kiss with a girl he just met. A girl he would end up falling in love with. He'd start doing everything she wanted to do, which of course meant giving up video games, since she'd be jealous of every moment he spent away from her.

They'd end up getting married and having children and they'd throw lavish parties where he'd bring up his old days as a comic-book-loving geek who played video games. And his friends—stockbrokers and lawyers, of course—would all laugh and laugh and relentlessly tease him, but all in good fun. And maybe he'd remember, as the subject changed back to sports, the girl he used to play with. The one who sat beside him on a virtual mountaintop, watching the sunset with him as he bared his soul. But of course he wouldn't bring her up because his wife would get annoyed and grumpy and he really didn't want to deal with that. So he'd jump into the sports conversation and forget all about Allora all over again.

Argh. I had to stop. I'd drive myself insane. If I wasn't already there.

If only I could meet him. I mean, who knew? We could turn out to have nothing in common. No chemistry. No sparks. The bond we shared online could be completely virtual and not hold up in the real world. It would, at least, break the spell he had over me and help me come to terms with the fact that Sir Leo was just another guy and not someone crazy special with magical powers to melt my heart. The angsty pain of unrequited love would fade and we could simply remain good friends who liked to play video games together.

Easier said than done.

Forcing it out of my mind, I glanced over at my sister, sound asleep on my bed. She looked like a little blond cherub, her thumb stuck securely in her mouth. As annoying as she could be at times, she really was a cute kid. And a good sister, too—risking Mom's wrath by not selling me out. Maybe there was hope for her yet.

I walked over and sat on the side of the bed, brushing a strand of hair from her face, and leaned down to kiss her on the top of her head.

Then I went downstairs to apologize to Grandma.

THURSDAY AT school, I came across Black Raven, rummaging through her locker, iPod headphones stuck in her multiple-pierced ears. I started to approach her, but then hung back, unsure. Would she be okay with my talking to her outside the manga club? Or would someone like me be bad for her rep?

I considered turning around and walking the other direction, but before I could make a move, she looked over and saw me. She grinned and pulled her headphones out of her ears, wrapping the cord around her neck to hold them in place. "Maddy!" she cried. "What's up, girl?"

I let out a breath, relieved, then scolded myself for being so paranoid. Of course she'd want to talk to *me*. It would be *the Haters* she'd deem unworthy of her time.

"Hey, Blackie," I greeted. "Um, you don't mind if I call you Blackie, do you? What are you up to?"

She laughed. "No, I don't mind. Some of my other friends do, too. Black Raven is a bit of a mouthful. Just as long as you don't call me Treena, we're golden." She closed her locker. "As for what I'm up to, I'm trying to survive the day so I can evacuate the premises and head downtown after school." She tossed her book bag over one shoulder. "Not that this lame city has a real downtown."

"Yeah," I said. "I know what you mean. I moved here from Boston and it's so different from what I'm used to."

Black Raven looked at me with something that actually resembled respect. "Dude," she cried. "You lived in Boston? I'm so jealous."

"Yeah, I miss it a lot. Especially my old school. This place isn't exactly . . . diverse."

"Yeah, the Killer Clones can be a bit much to take here," she said, gesturing to two students walking down the hall in identical T-shirts and khaki pants. They glared at her and she cheerfully waved.

I giggled. She was so cool. Confident in who she was. Not afraid to stand up to anyone. I bet the Haters didn't mess with her. I bet they didn't dare.

Which made her a perfect potential friend, I realized. Maybe I should ask her if she wanted to hang after school. I wouldn't mind joining her downtown—even if it was kind of lame.

Then again, a nagging voice in the back of my head pestered, *just because she's okay with talking to you in the halls doesn't mean she'll suddenly want to be BFFs. In fact, she's probably just humoring you 'cause you're president of the manga club or something.*

No. I shook my head. I had to stop this. Just because Billy

considered me a social leper didn't mean everyone did. And if I never took a chance, I was certain to be alone forever.

"So you're going downtown after school?" I asked.

She rolled her eyes. "Unfortunately," she said. "As there's zero entertainment in this town."

"Well, they do have Mel's Comics. They have a great manga selection," I reminded her. "If you wanted, I could tag along and we could see what's new."

I held my breath, waiting for the pause, the look of guilt, the internal debate on how she would squirm out of the proposal. Make some excuse as to why we couldn't hang out to hide the fact that she just didn't want to hang out with me.

But it never came.

Instead she nodded without hesitation, her green, almost catlike eyes shining. "Great idea," she said. "Want to meet me out in front of the school at the end of last period?"

"Sure. Sounds perfect. See you then." I gave her a small wave, then headed to my next class, forcing myself not to skip down the hallways like a first grader. For the first time since I'd come to this stupid school, I had actual social plans. I felt like bursting into song.

• • •

After an eternity of lectures, experiments, and pop quizzes, the final bell rang and the inmates were allowed to flee the jail. After stashing my books in my locker, I headed outside and found Black Raven sitting on the brick wall by the buses with a couple other kids. She saw me and waved me over.

"Hey, guys, this is my friend Maddy," she introduced me. "She draws the most amazing manga you've ever seen."

"Hi," I said, feeling myself blush. Friend. She called me friend. Sure, she might have been using the term loosely, but I'd take it anyway.

"Hey, Maddy," greeted a tall skinny skateboarder. He brushed his long stringy hair from his face. "How's it hanging?"

"Nice to meet you," said the pretty girl to his left. She wore a long flowing skirt and had flowers tucked into her pixie-cut blond hair. "I'm Amy and this is Trent. Blackie's been telling us all about your art."

I beamed.

"Yeah," added Trent. "We'd love to check it out."

Black Raven hopped off the wall. "No, no, not now, kiddies," she said. "There's no time for show-and-tell. Maddy and I have über-important plans we must attend to."

"Oh, fine," Trent mocked. "Offer her up, then steal her away again. Deprive us of the one shred of cultural relevance we might have gotten out of the school day."

"Why don't you come by our table at lunch tomorrow?" Amy suggested. "You can show us your manga then. We eat at the far left quadrant."

"Great. I definitely will," I said, trying to sound cool and not overly excited at the first offer of non-solo lunch since I'd gotten to this stupid school.

"Okay, okay already. She'll come to lunch. Jeez, you guys

are so demanding," Black Raven mocked. "Okay, we're out. Catch ya tomorrow."

"Bye! Nice to meet you," I cried as she grabbed me by the hand and yanked me away.

I followed Blackie down to the lower parking lot, forcing myself not to dance in happiness. *Be cool, Maddy,* I told myself. *Don't blow it.*

She reached into her bag and pulled out her keys, then gestured to the bright yellow Mini Cooper. "I'm obsessed with everything English," she explained. We got in and headed downtown. She reached down to turn up the stereo and—to my delight—soon the car was filled with the sounds of My Chemical Romance. We sang along with Gerard at the top of our lungs the whole way there and I suddenly realized I didn't have to worry about being cool. With someone like Black Raven I could just be me. That was enough.

Downtown consisted of one main street with cobblestone sidewalks and gas streetlamps that were supposed to give the place a charming, old-world look, reminiscent of colonial times. Most of the shops sold antiques or touristy odds and ends—nothing that would appeal to anyone under the age of sixty. Luckily, at the far end of the street, a guy named Mel had taken over his grandma's old yarn store and turned it into a comic book shop.

After chatting with Mel himself for a few moments, we started skimming through the racks, looking for new releases or rare finds, calling out to each other when we spotted something good. Blackie made me purchase the first volume of *Chibi Vampire* and I convinced her to give something non-fanged a try for once, introducing her to my beloved *Dramacon* series.

"The author of these—Svetlana Chmakova—is really amazing," I said, handing her volumes one and two. "And the coolest thing is, she's the VIP judge for that contest I told you about."

"Oh, yeah." Blackie nodded, remembering. "What's the deal with that, anyway?"

"Well, for the first round of judging, I go to the Boston Public Library and present my book to a panel of judges."

"In person? Yikes."

"Yeah. And I'm totally freaking out," I said. "I mean, especially since Svetlana's going to be there. What if she doesn't like my drawings or says they're totally amateur? She could be, like, 'Wow, girl, you need to give up drawing and take up accounting instead.'"

Black Raven giggled. "Yeah, right," she said. "I doubt they're allowed to say that. And besides, your drawings rock. I bet you'll win, hands down."

I crossed my fingers and held them up. She did the same.

"Okay, I'm dying of thirst. Let's buy these bad boys and grab a snack at the diner."

"Sounds like a plan."

"Hey, isn't that Matt Drewer over there?" Blackie asked, pointing down the aisle to the Marvel section.

I followed her finger. Sure enough, there was Matt, flipping through a bin of comics. "Oh, yeah. We should say hi," I said, heading down the aisle. After all, he was one of the few nice students in Hannah Dustin High. "Hey, Matt," I greeted.

"Hey, girls!" he said, looking happy to see us. "Guess we had the same idea, huh? Whatcha buying?"

"Shojo." Blackie held up her selections. "Maddy's trying to cure me of my vampire addiction."

"And Blackie's trying to get me addicted," I answered back, holding up *Chibi Vampire*.

"Very nice," he said, giving me a thumbs-up. "I came here to find *Fullmetal Alchemist*. I really dug what we read during the meeting." He grinned. "You may turn me into a manga fan yet, Maddy."

I laughed appreciatively. "Hey, we're going to grab some food. Want to come?"

Matt shrugged. "Sure. Why not?"

We paid for our books and headed across the street to the local diner. It was a fifties-themed place with records on the wall and photos of Elvis everywhere. Each table had its own jukebox, but we quickly decided none of the old-school selections were worth the quarter price tag. We ordered sodas and then pulled out our purchases and spread them out over the table.

"You're really going to love *Chibi Vampire*," Black Raven told me. "It's so good."

"And you're going to love . . ." I trailed off, my eyes catching sight of Chad Murray, sitting in a booth at the far end of the restaurant, alone and reading, a cup of coffee sitting in front of him.

"What?" Black Raven demanded, looking in my direction. "Ah, one of the sheep has strayed from the heard. We should attack now, while it's alone and helpless."

Matt snorted. "Totally."

I swatted at them, straining to see what Chad was reading. Probably a *Sports Illustrated* swimsuit issue or something. "You guys are terrible."

"For making fun of the Haters, as you call them?" Matt scoffed. "Puh-leeze. They so deserve that and more."

"Maybe. Though maybe not Chad. He's okay, actually. When he's not around Billy."

Blackie raised an eyebrow. "Are you crazy?" she asked. "He's one of the inner circle!"

"I know. It's just . . . well, I think he may be different from the rest." I shrugged. It sounded lame when I said it out loud.

"Ohhh, I get it," Black Raven said with a knowing voice. She giggled and poked Matt. He snorted in return. I turned back to look at them, puzzled. "Get what?"

"You like him." Blackie's eyes danced in merriment.

I felt my face go bright red. "I do not."

"Mmm-hmm."

"I DON'T!"

Matt chimed in. "Maddy and Chaddy sitting in a tree, K-I-S-S—"

"Shhh," I cried, putting hand over her mouth. We tussled for a bit, until the waitress came over with our sodas and told us we needed to settle down.

"Sorry, Gladys," Black Raven said, immediately in polite mode.

"You always are, Blackie," Gladys said, shaking her head. She was heavyset and in her fifties, with purple eye shadow dusted on her eyelids. "And yet every time you come here you manage to annoy me all over again."

"That's why you love me so much."

Gladys snorted. "I could think of another word."

"I'm sure you could. You're a regular thesaurus. But seriously, Gladys, can you do me a huge favor? Like the hugest favor in the entire universe?"

"And what, pray tell, would that favor entail?"

Blackie grinned. "Would you ask that gentleman at the far table if he would care to join us?"

"What!?" I cried, horrified. "No!"

Of course my new friend ignored me, fluttering her fake eyelashes at our waitress instead.

Gladys rolled her eyes. "The things I do for you kids," she muttered. She left our table and headed over to Chad's. I watched as the two of them started to converse.

"I can't believe you just did that!" I squeal-whispered, looking back at my friends. "What if he comes over?"

Black Raven rolled her eyes. "Then you talk to him, dummy. That's kind of the point."

"But he's . . . he's one of them."

"You just told me he was different. So let's find out if you're right."

"He won't come. He's totally not going to come. . . ." I clamped my mouth shut as I watched Chad stand up and shove his belongings in his bag. Was he really going to . . . ?

"See, here he is!" Black Raven pronounced triumphantly. I didn't know whether I wanted to kill her or hug her.

"Hey," Chad said when he arrived at our table. He shifted from foot to foot and shot me a small, uncomfortable smile. "How's it going?"

"Would you like to sit down?" Black Raven asked in her sweetest voice. She threw her book bag on the seat next to her. "There's plenty of room next to *Maddy*."

If you could die of humiliation, I'd be a goner for sure.

"Sure," Chad said, sitting down beside me. As he did, his knee touched mine under the table and I jerked back, as if I had been struck by extremely high voltage. It was inhuman how this boy affected me.

"You okay?" he asked, looking concerned. "Did I . . . kick you or something?"

"She's fine," Black Raven answered for me. "So, Chad, come here often?"

He laughed. He had such a nice laugh. So . . . merry.

Oh, wow, I sounded like a Christmas carol. Shoot me now.

"As a matter of fact, I do," he said. "I like it here. It's nice and quiet and I don't have to deal with anyone from school."

He blushed as he realized what he was saying. "Well, I mean, anyone I don't want to deal with. Not you guys, of course."

"Don't worry, we know exactly who you mean," Matt said. "What we don't know is why you hang out with those tools to begin with."

Chad stared down at his lap, looking embarrassed. "We've been friends since kindergarten," he said with a shrug. "I don't know."

"Yeah, well, that's like ten years too long in my opinion," Blackie piped in. "I mean, loyalty is one thing. But do you know what you're doing to your reputation by hanging out with those guys? Everyone thinks you're just like the rest of them."

"But I'm not." Chad looked pained. "I'm nothing like them."

"So says Maddy. I say, guilt by association," Matt declared. "But hey, what do you care? You're one of the most popular kids in school. Doesn't matter what freaks like us think, right?"

"That's not fair!" Chad retorted. "I don't care at all about that popularity stuff. I never have. Seriously. And I never pick on anyone."

"Sure, you may not pick on anyone yourself," I blurted out, suddenly angry. Visions of him shuffling his feet and staying silent while his best friend made my life a living hell over and over again swirled in my head. "But you don't exactly stop your friends from doing it either. I mean, how about using your popularity power for good for once in your life instead of sticking your head in the sand while your friends torment and torture people on a daily basis?"

I stopped shouting, realizing everyone at the table was staring at me. Wow, where had that outburst come from? I think I surprised even myself. But it needed to be said and I wasn't going to take it back now. I was sick of being the victim. And while I might not have magical powers like my *Gamer Girl* heroine, I could and would stand up for myself from this point on.

Chad was quiet for a moment, probably as shocked as everyone else. Then he nodded slowly. "You're right," he said. "You're totally right." He looked up at me. "I'm sorry, Maddy. You deserve better." He met my eyes with his own beautiful blue ones and I swallowed hard at the sudden tension between us. As angry as I was, he still had the power to turn my insides to mush. "Next time I'll do something. I promise."

"I'll hold you to that," I said, forcing myself to laugh and lighten the mood.

"I hope so." He looked so earnest, for a moment I thought he was going to kiss me. But that was stupid. He may have agreed to back me when his friends got out of line, but that didn't mean he was head over heels in love.

Matt cleared his throat and rose from his seat. "It's been real," he said, throwing himself into a gallant bow. "But I must be going now."

"What? So soon?" Blackie asked. "We haven't even bribed Gladys for an extra-large slice of blueberry pie yet."

"I'm sorry, but blueberry pie must wait. I have a hot date that cannot."

"Ooh," I said teasingly, mostly to get him back for the Chad thing. "Who with?"

He blushed. "Actually, it's an online date."

I looked up, startled. Was everyone meeting people online these days?

Blackie high-fived Matt. "Nice," she said. "Someone around here?"

"Don't know. Don't care." Matt shrugged, then grinned. "All I know is I am in L-O-V-E." He dug into his pocket and threw down some money. "Later, guys."

I glanced down at my watch, startled when I realized how late it was. We'd been having such a good time I'd lost track. I was supposed to meet Sir Leo in less than a half hour. My own online date . . .

I blinked, a horrible thought coming to me. I glanced across the restaurant, watching Matt's retreating figure through the swinging door.

It couldn't be.

Could it?

My mind started racing, connecting the dots. Matt lived in Farmingdale. Matt was in drama. Matt had a love for comic books. Matt just met a girl online and was supposed to meet her tonight.

What if Matt was Sir Leo?

My stomach dropped out from under me. Much like when you go on that Tower of Terror ride at Disney and barrel thirteen stories down in an out-of-control elevator. Was Matt Sir Leo? Was Sir Leo Matt?

It couldn't be. And yet . . . it totally could.

No, I told myself. It was just a coincidence. A crazy coincidence. There was no way my beautiful, dashing knight in shining armor was Matt Drewer. Could there?

"Maddy, you okay?" Blackie asked, peering at me.

"Yeah, you look really pale," Chad said, reaching over to feel my forehead with his hand. "Are you coming down with something?"

I shook my head, trying to ignore the tingles his touch sent through my body. That was the reaction I wanted to get from a real-life Sir Leo. The kind of reaction I'd never ever get from a guy like Matt, no matter what a nice person he was.

"I'm fine," I said, rising from my seat. "But I've got to get going before Mom has a fit." I squeezed out of the booth and dropped a couple of bucks on the table. "I'll catch you later."

WHAT DO you mean you aren't coming?" Mom barked into the phone.

It was Saturday morning, ten o'clock. Two full hours after the time Dad was supposed to come pick us up. Mom had been calling his cell every five minutes, but hadn't gotten anything but voice mail up until now.

"I don't care how tired you are. You get in the car and come pick up your children. They've been waiting for you."

Emily dropped her Sleeping Beauty suitcase on the hallway flagstone and let out a small sigh. I knew exactly how she felt.

"I have to work, Bob. I can't just drop everything because you're feeling lazy."

I leaned against the wall, closing my eyes. Great. This was just great. I had actually been looking forward to this weekend, too. Dad had promised to take Emily and me snowboarding. We were going to meet up with Caitlin, Ashley, Dana—even David Silverman. All my old Boston friends.

We'd been planning it over e-mail all week. Where we'd meet up. What trails we'd snowboard on. Everything. It would be the first time I'd had a chance to meet up with my old friends since I left Boston.

But Dad hadn't shown up that morning. At first, I'd been worried. Maybe he'd gotten into an accident on the way over. Or his apartment burned down. Or he had hit his head somehow and was even now lying in a hospital with amnesia.

Even Mom seemed a little nervous by her fifteenth unanswered call. I'd kept peering out the window, looking for his SUV to turn the corner and praying he was okay.

Good news—he was okay.

Bad news—it didn't look like our ski trip was happening.

"You haven't changed a bit, have you?" Mom accused. "Still making those promises you can't seem to keep." She white-knuckled the receiver. "It's one thing to disappoint me, but these are your children."

"We're not going skiing, are we?" Emily asked, looking up at me with sad blue eyes.

I shook my head, my heart aching. "Don't think it's likely," I said. I reached down to grab her small hand in mine. "Come on," I said, "let's go watch cartoons."

But Grandma was watching some sort of History Channel program when we went into the living room and wasn't about to hand over the remote. So Emily and I ended up upstairs, each heading to our own room. I lay down on my bed, staring up at the ceiling.

A knock sounded on my door. "Come in," I called out.

Mom appeared, her eyes red and watery. Great. "Hi, sweetie," she said, walking over to the bed. "Are you okay?"

"Sure," I said, looking back up at the ceiling. In my old room, back in Boston, I'd pasted glow-in-the-dark stars up there. I wondered if the new people had kept them or if they'd torn them all down and thrown them away. It shouldn't matter, I supposed. Not like I'd ever be back there. But in a way, it did.

I'd asked Grandma when we'd first moved in if I could put new stars on my ceiling here. She'd acted as if I'd suggested bringing in a sledgehammer and smashing down a wall to make room for a raging nightclub. Mom told me later that Grandma was "set in her ways," which was one way to put it. "A stubborn old mule" would be another.

Mom sat down on the edge of my bed. "Your dad had . . . something come up," she explained. "He's . . . sick. So he can't take you skiing today after all."

"Um, yeah. I figured that."

"He feels very bad about it. . . ."

"Right."

Mom sighed. "I've got to go to work. Can you watch your sister for the afternoon?"

"Sure. Whatever."

"I'm sorry, Maddy. I really am. I know you were looking forward to the trip."

"Really. It's no big deal." Of course my voice chose to

crack on "no," pretty much cementing the fact that it actually *was* one. Great. The last thing I wanted to do was to give Mom more reasons to be mad at Dad. I swallowed hard. *Play it cool, Maddy.* "Actually, it works out well," I added. "I didn't really feel like snowboarding today anyway."

Mom gave me a pitying look that told me she didn't buy my brave act for one millisecond. Not surprising, I guess; I was a terrible actress. She glanced at her watch. "God, I'm so late," she muttered. "Sorry, I've got to go. I'll see you tonight. Maybe we can get something special for dinner. Go out to Longhorn's or something," she suggested, naming my favorite steak place. She was trying, I'd give her that.

"Sounds good," I said, without much enthusiasm.

Mom exited my room, shutting the door behind her. I thought about Caitlin and the gang, in the ski lodge waiting for me at our meeting spot right this very second. How long would they hang before they realized I wasn't coming? There wasn't even a way to contact them, seeing as the cell phones didn't work in the mountains.

This was not good. I rolled over to my side and pulled my knees up to my chest, fetal position. Then I pulled the covers over my head, wanting to hide from the world. Might as well go back to bed—nothing else going on today. All I could say was, Dad better have the plague to let us down like this.

I lay in bed for a few minutes tossing and turning restlessly, but my mind refused to calm down and let me sleep. There was too much to think about. The manga club. The

Haters. Dad. Fields of Fantasy. Sir Leo. Matt maybe being Sir Leo.

I hadn't logged into the game Thursday night like I was supposed to when I got home from hanging out with Blackie, Chad, and Matt. I was too upset about the possibility of Sir Leo actually being Matt Drewer and didn't know how to face him. I tried to tell myself it wasn't a bad thing to have Sir Leo turn out to be a nice normal guy and not someone horrible like Billy or something. Matt was funny. Smart. Interesting. I should be happy to have him be Sir Leo.

But I wasn't. Not by a long shot. In fact, I was downright miserable. Because let's be honest here. I didn't want Sir Leo to be just some random funny, smart, interesting guy. I wanted Sir Leo to be my knight in shining armor. A guy who made my heart pitter-patter like crazy when I laid eyes on him. Like Chad did. I wanted to swoon like the heroines in Grandma's romance novels were always doing. I wanted to close my eyes and feel his sweet breath on my face as he leaned down to press his soft lips to mine.

That wasn't going to happen with Matt. It just wasn't.

Still, an inner voice nagged, *don't you think you're being a little unfair? Sir Leo's been your loyal and faithful friend for a while now. It's not right to ditch him simply because he's not a love connection.*

It was a good point. And what else did I have to do but waste time on the computer, now that my weekend was shot? I got out of bed, signed into the game, and did a search for Sir Leo.

He wasn't on. But someone else was. Someone who was supposedly sooo sick he couldn't take his two darling daughters to the mountains.

[Allora] Dad?
[RockStarBob] Oh, hi, sweetie. How's it going?

I narrowed my eyes as I read his words. That was it? No apology? No "I'm sorry I let you down. I'm a miserable excuse for a father. Please forgive me and I'll make it up to you with many, many presents in the near future"? Just an "Oh, hi, sweetie," as if he hadn't ruined my whole weekend?

I had to get to the bottom of this.

[Allora] I'm fine. You know, for being stuck at home and not snowboarding.
[RockStarBob] Um, yeah. Sorry about that. I wasn't feeling well.
[Allora] I heard Mom say you were sick. . . .
[RockStarBob] Right. Been throwing up all morning.
[Allora] Ugh. Way TMI, Dad.

I took in breath. Well, that was good, right? I mean, not that he was suffering from food poisoning, of course, but at least he had a real excuse. I wouldn't want to drive two hours north to ski country if I was barfing either. Couldn't really blame him for that, I supposed.

[Allora] Well, did you want to play then? I mean since we can't hang out in person.

I waited for his response, but none came. At first I thought he might have disconnected, but then finally his IM popped up on my screen.

[RockStarBob] Um, sorry, hon. Not right now. I'm supposed to do this huge raid with a bunch of guys. We're going to infiltrate the enemy city of Kalgar.
[Allora] Oh.
[RockStarBob] Sorry, sweetie. We've been planning this for weeks.

What?! What did he just say? He didn't say that, did he?

[Allora] Planning it for weeks?????????

There was no immediate answer. Not shocking, I supposed, seeing as he'd just been totally busted. Suddenly all the puzzle pieces fit into place. He'd blown off our real-life plans to go skiing because his online friends wanted him to raid. Evidently disappointing his daughters was a lot easier than letting down his gamer buds.

What a jerk. What a total jerk. I glared at the computer screen, trying to resist the overwhelming urge to put my fist through it. If there was a way to do it and hurt him on the other side, I would have definitely tried.

[RockStarBob] Er, right. What I meant to say is that we'd been planning to raid for weeks. Not necessarily today, though. It just ended up working out that way because I was home sick.

Jerk. He was a total jerk. How could he do that to us? Stand us up? Leave us hanging? He didn't even have the nerve to cancel. Mom had to track him down to get the scoop. He'd probably stayed up real late and had forgotten to set his alarm—after all, he'd never planned to make the ski trip to begin with.

I ached as I thought about Emily's sad face. Mom's fury. My friends, wandering the resort, wondering where I was. Me, missing out on that last chance to keep some connection with them.

So selfish. So, so selfish.

[RockStarBob] Are you still there, honey? You're not mad, are you?
[Allora] I'm fine.
[RockStarBob] Cool. That's my girl. I knew you'd understand—after all, you're a gamer, too! So I'll TTYL, kk?

I gritted my teeth in frustration. A gamer. Please. A real gamer understood when it was time to shut down the game. A real gamer knew when life came first.

Yes, I was a gamer. My dad, on the other hand, was merely a computer addict. His precious online world had become more important to him than his day-to-day existence. And he'd proven time and time again that he'd abandon those who needed him if it meant more time in front of the computer screen. No wonder Mom had left him.

I switched off the computer without bothering to answer or say good-bye. Not that he'd notice.

I pulled out my manga project and started drawing furiously, pouring my heart and soul out into my art. I sketched the scene. Allora, back in the real world, back in school. The bullies who once plagued her relentlessly catch sight of her and stop her in the hallway, jeering and calling her a freak, just like they used to before she went into the game. They throw spitballs at her and pull her hair and rip her dress. But this time Allora doesn't cringe and cry and try to run away like she once would have. This time Allora simply stretches out her arms and raises her hands. Suddenly bolts of lightning shoot from her fingers, crackling into the air. The bullies scream, wetting their pants with fear before they turn tail and run away. The other kids cheer. She's their hero. Allora nods smugly. She knows it's good to be Gamer Girl.

I smiled down at the drawing. My sad, helpless freak girl had put her newfound powers to use. She'd become confident and not afraid to face life head-on. I was proud of her.

I looked over at my abandoned snowboard still leaning by the door.

What would Gamer Girl do in a situation like this?

It suddenly seemed very obvious.

Minutes later, I was downstairs. "So, Grandma," I said, smiling. "Can I ask you a favor?"

• • •

I'm not going to say it didn't take some pretty pathetic begging and pleading, but not a half hour later, Emily and I were in the car with Grandma, driving toward the mountains. She had been surprisingly agreeable to the suggestion. Well, after I offered to dust her entire unicorn collection, anyway, which was going to take me years to finish. But it'd be worth it—especially after seeing Emily's ecstatic face when I told her we were going after all.

We arrived around lunchtime and found my friends in the lodge, surrounded by piles of food. They screamed and squealed when they saw us and immediately plied us with hot chocolate and pizza. (Much to Emily's delight.) We found Grandma a cozy armchair by a fireplace and she settled in with a romance novel while we hit the slopes. Emily joined other eight-year-olds for a lesson and my friends and I headed over to the park, navigating the jumps and rails as best we could. Caitlin was still learning, so she took the side routes, cheering us on as we attempted various tricks.

"It's good to have you with us again," Caitlin remarked as we rode up the chairlift together. "I've missed you, you know."

I rubbed my mittens together to stay warm. "I've missed you guys, too."

"So is your new school still totally lame?" Caitlin asked. "I bet all those Aberzombies make it completely unbearable."

I started to reply, then thought about it for a moment. "You know," I said, surprising myself. "I think it's growing on me. The school, that is. Not the Aberzombies."

Caitlin laughed appreciatively. "Well, that's good."

"Yeah." I nodded. "I mean it's not as good as Boston Academy by any means. But it's not all bad either. I actually started a manga club last week and a ton of people showed up. It was pretty awesome."

"Really? Like we were doing before you left?"

"Sort of. But this one's an official school club. And I'm the club president."

"That's so cool," Caitlin squealed. "I tried to get our club approved by B.A. after you left, but the principal totally denied us. He said we should start a Shakespeare club or something instead."

I started laughing. "A Shakespeare club? For real?"

"Uh, yeah. I couldn't make up something that lame if I tried." Caitlin shook her head mournfully. "I'm totally jealous you got yours pushed through."

"Yeah, it's pretty great," I agreed, thinking back to our first meeting. "And it's got a lot of potential. We're even talking about a club trip to New York Comic Con."

"Wow, that'd be amazing," Caitlin said. "I'm going to have

to stow away in your luggage for that." She looked over at me and smiled. "I'm so happy for you, Maddy. You seem much better, too. Less . . . I don't know . . . emo, or something."

"Yeah," I admitted. "I guess I am."

· · ·

Mom had steaming bowls of clam chowder waiting for us when we got home. She and Grandma sat at the table as we ate them, asking about our trip. We gave them play-by-plays, laughing at the misadventures.

After dinner, I headed up to my room. I considered working more on my manga, but I was too exhausted. I decided to sign on to Fields of Fantasy instead.

As soon as I signed on, I got a whisper from Dad.

[RockStarBob] Hey, sweetie! Good to see you back. I'm done raiding now if you want to go do something.

I frowned. Ah, now it was convenient for him. So I should just forgive and forget what happened earlier, right? Whatever. I ignored him and messaged Sir Leo instead.

[Allora] Greetings, Sir Leo. How dost thou fare this fine evening?
[SirLeo] Very well, m'lady. Even better since you are here!

I sighed. The thrill I used to feel when he said such sweet things had totally evaporated. Now I could only imagine

them coming from Matt, which did nothing for me whatsoever except make me feel guilty.

Ugh. What was wrong with me? Why couldn't I accept
that my knight was a real-life really nice guy? I should be
psyched. And yet all I could feel was shallow and selfish and
totally not into Matt.

[SirLeo] (How was skiing with your dad?)

[Allora] (Actually my dad didn't go.)

[SirLeo] (??)

[Allora] (Yeah, he's too much of a video game addict to get
up from the computer and go outside. Sun might kill him or
something.)

[SirLeo] (Aw, that stinks. I'm so sorry. I know you were
really looking forward to that.)

[Allora] (Yeah, I was. So we went without him. Had to bribe
Grandma, but it was totally worth it.)

[SirLeo] (Nice. I'm so glad you still got to go.)

[Allora] (Me, too.)

[SirLeo] (What did you say to your dad?)

[Allora] (He messaged me when I first logged on, but I
ignored him.)

[SirLeo] (Hmm.)

[Allora] (?)

[SirLeo] (You should probably talk to him, you know.)

[Allora] (Heh. Yeah.)

[SirLeo] (I'm serious. Otherwise, this kind of stuff may start
happening all the time. And you don't want that, do you?)

[Allora] (Definitely not. You're right.)

[SirLeo] (LOL, I'm always right. Haven't you learned that by now?)

[Allora] (Yes, yes. LOL.)

I considered his words for a moment. Maybe I *should* confront Dad. Let him know how selfish he was, and how it felt to be ditched. Maybe he didn't even realize it was such a big deal.

[Allora] (Well, thanks for the advice. Maybe I'll do that. What are you up to, anyway?)

[SirLeo] (Well, this morn I hit the comic book store and got the latest *X-Men*.)

[Allora] (Nice.)

He went back to the comic store again? After we saw him there on Thursday? Wow. He was seriously into it. Or maybe we'd interrupted his shopping with our food invitation and he hadn't picked up everything he'd gone for.

[SirLeo] (Oh, and I picked up some manga, too. Good idea. Love it so far.)

[Allora] (What did you get?)

[SirLeo] (Ummm . . . The latest Fruit Baskets.)

I cocked my head in confusion. Hang on a second, wasn't that . . . ?

[Allora] (Isn't that a little . . . I don't know . . . girlie?)

[SirLeo] (ROFL. Yes. I Wikipedia'd it just to freak you out. Just kidding, of course.)

[Allora] (LOL. What did you get really?)

[SirLeo] (*Naruto* and *Hellsing*.)

[Allora] (Ah. Much more manly. Never read those.)

[SirLeo] (That's 'cause you're a grrrrly grrrl.)

[Allora] (!! Whatev. I could still take you down in a duel.)

Sir Leo shivers.

[SirLeo] Sorry, m'lady. I promise to show more respect for thee in the future.

[Allora] He-he. That's better.

I lapsed into our old banter without meaning to. It was so hard. He still acted and talked exactly like Sir Leo. The guy I was in love with online. It was hard to remember he was really Matt behind the character.

Well, *maybe* it was Matt. I still wasn't positive, of course. For all I knew the similarities could all be a total coincidence. After all, Farmingdale was a popular name for a town. He could be from Farmingdale, New York, not New Hampshire. Or Farmingdale, Maine. Or Farmingdale—

[SirLeo] (Oh! I totally forgot to tell you. They started a manga club at my school.)

Then again, he could be Matt from Farmingdale, New Hampshire, the school where they just started a manga club this week.

> **[SirLeo]** (This new girl at our school named Maddy started it. She's really cool. Into manga just like you. She was giving me some suggestions after school on Thursday.)

My heart sank. There was no use denying things any longer. Sir Leo was Matt. Matt was Sir Leo. Definitely. Without a doubt. I stared at the screen, not knowing what to type back. Should I let him know who I was?

> **[SirLeo]** M'lady? Where did you wander off to?
> **[Allora]** (Sorry. Mom's calling me. I've got to go. Catch you later.)
> **[SirLeo]** (Oh. Um, okay . . . Later, I guess.)
> ***SirLeo signs off.***

Wow, I was such a wimp. What was wrong with me? I should have just told him who I was. It was the perfect opening and I'd messed it up.

I switched off the computer, feeling like dirt. If only things had turned out differently. If only Sir Leo had turned out to be a real-life knight in shining armor, too. But no. I just wasn't that lucky.

My phone started ringing. Caller ID told me it was Dad. I thought about just ignoring it, but I knew I had to face him eventually. Might as well get it over with while I was already in a bad mood.

"Hey, Dad."

"Maddy, how are you?" He sounded happy to hear my voice. "I tried to message you in-game a little bit ago, but you didn't answer."

"Sorry. I must have been afk . . ." I trailed off, realizing there was no point in lying. "Actually, I saw your message. I was just ignoring you."

The other end went quiet. Then he said, "I see."

"I know. I should have answered. I was just . . . well, I'm kinda mad at you," I blurted out. "You totally blew us off—your own kids—for your stupid video games." I wasn't about to tell him that we'd figured out a way to go without him. That would let him off the hook and I wanted him dangling.

"I know. I'm sorry," Dad said with a long sigh. "I messed up."

"Yes, you did. And not only that, you had the nerve to lie to me about it."

"I didn't—"

"Didn't lie?" I scoffed. "Okay, are you sick, then? Lying in bed needing chicken soup? Should I send a doctor over?"

"No, but, I—"

"Or did you just say you were sick 'cause you forgot we had plans and had made arrangements to go raiding with your online friends?"

"Well, I mean . . ." Dad spluttered. "I really wasn't feeling very good this morning. . . ."

"A hangover doesn't count, Dad."

Silence. Then, "When did you get so grown-up, Maddy?"

"Dad, Emily and I love you. And we want to hang out with you and stuff. But you can't cancel on us like that. It's not fair. We're people, too, you know."

"I know, I know. I'm sorry. I really am," Dad said, sounding very upset. "I promise to make it up to you. Next weekend we'll do something really special, I promise."

"Okay . . ."

"Seriously. I swear."

"I believe you," I assured him. "And I'm looking forward to it."

I hung up the phone, feeling much better already. Sir Leo was right—it was better just to come clean. Too bad I couldn't do the same with him.

18

I THINK we're going to need more chairs!"

Ms. Reilly smiled as she scanned the library for additional seating. Wednesday, week two of the manga club, and it was packed to capacity. At least twenty people lounged around the table, chowing on pizza and talking animatedly to one another.

I studied each new member closely, wondering who they were and why they had decided to join the club. There seemed to be no common denominator—with every school clique represented. From art geeks to prom queens.

"Great turnout," Matt noted, nudging me in the elbow.

I gave him a small smile, feeling totally guilty. I wondered if he noticed I'd been avoiding him in the halls and had been "too busy" to log into the game all week. I knew I was being a total wimp and should just deal with it and confront him, rather than let it eat away at me and make me miserable, but I couldn't help it.

"Nervous?" Ed asked from across the table.

"Definitely." I looked down at my notes. I had expected to give my little "How to Draw Manga" session to a handful of kids. Not half of Hannah Dustin High. "Maybe we should postpone it for another week or something. . . ."

"No way," Blackie chimed in from my right. "You are so not backing out now."

"Yeah," Jessie agreed. "I want to learn to draw and you said you'd teach us. And it would be completely unfair and not cool for you to change your mind now and leave us totally art-challenged and stuff."

"Agreed," Ed said. "I had to trek all the way to the art room to get the sketchbooks and pencils. And you know how I hate to burn unnecessary calories."

I held up my hands in protest, laughing. "Okay, okay!" I cried. "You win. I'll teach." I couldn't help feeling secretly delighted at their encouragement.

"Was she trying to back out?" Ms. Reilly asked my friends. They all nodded in sync.

"Of course we didn't let her," Jessie assured the teacher. "After all, she is the best artist at Hannah Dustin and it would be very selfish of her to keep her talents to herself, don't you agree, Ms. Reilly?"

The teacher grinned. "I do." She turned to me. "So I'm going to do a little introduction and then hand things over to you."

I looked out at the audience, my heart pounding in my chest. "Okay . . ." I said.

Black Raven reached over to squeeze my hand. "Don't worry," she said, "you'll be fine. Better than fine. I daresay, you will be awesome."

"Agreed," said David. Jessie and Ed gave me thumbs-up.

"Thanks, guys," I replied, looking at them gratefully.

I smiled to myself, looking around the room at all the new faces, intermingled with more familiar ones. School had sure changed over the last week. Between Blackie and her crowd and the rest of the manga club members, I actually had a widening circle of friends at Hannah Dustin High. People to sit with at lunch and say hi to in the hallways. People to hang out with after school. It was a whole new world and I had to admit, even though I still missed Boston, I was beginning to like it here.

Suddenly a hush fell over the room and I noticed everyone was staring at the library entrance. I looked over and my jaw dropped to see Chad Murray and about seven other kids walk into the library.

"Is this the manga club?" Chad asked.

"Yes," Ms. Reilly said, beaming. "Yes, it is. Though we're running out of chairs. So some of you might have to just sit on the floor."

"Sorry," Chad said, wearing an embarrassed smile. "Matt was going on and on about the club in drama practice and we all decided we should check it out."

"The more the merrier," Ms. Reilly pronounced. "And it's a good day for you guys to come. Maddy, our club president, is going to give us all a lesson in drawing."

I could feel the blood drain from my face. "I feel sick," I whispered to Black Raven.

She grinned wickedly. "Aw, Maddy's boyfriend came to watch her," she teased.

"Shh! He is so not my boyfriend."

"Mmm-hmm. Then why's he here?"

"An undying desire to explore the mysteries that make up Japanese artwork?"

Black Raven rolled her eyes.

I stole a peek over at Chad and his friends. They all had settled in, cross-legged on the library rug, and were passing around some of the comics and graphic novels people had brought in. He caught my eye and gave me a thumbs-up.

Did he really like me? Was it possible? And if so, what would I do about it? At least I didn't have the Sir Leo conflict anymore. Not that it was really ever a conflict.

Something nagged at my insides. Something sad. I glanced over at Matt, who was chatting merrily with Ed. Truth be told, I'd missed Fields of Fantasy and adventuring with Sir Leo the past few days. I missed my sweet and gentle knight. How he'd ask about my day and really listen to my answer. Silly one moment, supportive the next.

How could it be? How could I be so completely in love with Sir Leo online and not feel even the slightest interest in real-life Matt? It was so unfair.

"Um, Maddy? Earth to Maddy?" Blackie waved a hand in front of my face. "Time for some art lessons, sistah."

I blushed. "Um, sorry," I said. I looked out over the room.

At all the eager faces, ready to learn how to draw. I stood up from my seat and walked over to the easel Ms. Reilly had set up at the front of the room and pulled the cap off my marker.

"Hi, all," I said. "I'm Maddy Starr and I'm going to teach you to draw manga."

Everyone put away your books, the midterm is about to begin." Thursday morning in chemistry class and Mr. Wilks passed a stack of test packets to each front row student, who took one, then passed the stack to the person seated behind him. I grabbed mine and skimmed through the questions, glad I'd studied so hard. Sure, it was mostly because I was trying to avoid signing into the computer and facing Matt/ Sir Leo, but hey, nice that my grades would benefit as a bonus to my chickenness.

I could feel eyes on me and turned to my left to see that Billy had seated himself directly next to me. He caught me looking and stuck out his tongue in greeting. I turned back to my test. I wasn't going to let him upset me right before an important exam.

"Good luck, Freak Girl," Billy whispered.

"I don't need luck, Idiot Boy," I retorted. "I studied."

"Everyone, quiet. This is not a shared learning experience," Mr. Wilks ordered, sitting down at his desk and opening up a copy of some best-selling spy thriller. "Anyone caught talking will be asked to leave the classroom."

The room fell quiet. I started marking my test, answering questions about chemicals and their appropriate symbols and what they'd become if mixed together. The exam was pretty straightforward, luckily. No trick questions. No stuff that wasn't in the book. For once, I was glad of my teacher's lack of creativity.

"Hey! Psst!" I could hear Billy whisper to my left. At first I figured he had to be addressing someone else. Probably some poor sap who'd allowed him to cheat off her test. Until, that was, he poked me with the eraser side of his pencil. "Hey, Freak Girl," he hissed. "I'm talking to you!"

"Don't call me that," I hissed. I looked over at Mr. Wilks's desk. Luckily, the teacher looked pretty engrossed in his book.

"Ooh, I'm sorry." Billy grinned, not looking the least bit apologetic. "What did you get for number three?" he asked.

"Your mother," I muttered, turning back to my test. He had some nerve, assuming I'd help him. I wouldn't have allowed my best friend to cheat off me, never mind some jerk like him.

"Aw, come on. Don't be like that. I gotta pass this stupid thing or I'll be kicked off the basketball team."

"Poor baby." As if I cared. I started working on the next question.

"Come on. Just let me see. . . ." He reached over and tried to angle my paper so he could read my answers. Furious, I jammed my elbow into his arm.

"Ow!" he cried loudly. Suddenly the entire class had their eyes on us. I cringed. This was not going to end well for me, I could feel it.

Mr. Wilks looked up, eyes narrowing. "What's going on here?" he demanded.

"She's trying to copy off me," Billy piped up immediately. "And when I didn't let her, she hit me."

"Oh, give me a break!" I cried. I couldn't believe he had the nerve to try to get the teacher to buy such a lie. After all, there were probably five other students who could attest to the fact that . . .

I looked behind me. At the ones who could defend me. Lucy. Chelsea. Chad. A chorus line of Haters.

Great.

"Mr. Wilks?" Lucy chimed in, waving a well-manicured hand in the air. Her silver bangle bracelets flashed under the fluorescent light. "I saw her do it."

"Me too," Chelsea added confidently. "And it's not surprising either. After all, she hates Billy. Remember when she hit him in the cafeteria?"

Oh, great. Now that was going to come back and haunt me, too.

"She's a menace to our school," Billy said, giving me a disgusted look. "She ought to be expelled."

Mr. Wilks got out of his chair and walked over to my

desk. "Young lady," he said, staring down at me with his beady eyes. "Obviously detention has not straightened you out. We don't tolerate cheating and we certainly don't tolerate violence here at Hannah Dustin. I want you to go see Principal Miller. I'm going to recommend that you be suspended."

"It's about time," Chelsea exclaimed, followed by murmurs of agreement from her friends.

My heart sank. Suspension? Mom would kill me if I got suspended. Not to mention it would go on my permanent record. It could screw up my chances of getting into a good college. Especially if they wrote down that I had cheated to boot.

"I didn't do anything!" I retorted, feeling the lump rise to my throat. I chocked it back. *Don't cry. Whatever you do, don't cry.*

Mr. Wilks frowned. "You've got two witnesses saying otherwise."

"But they're Billy's friends," I protested. "Not exactly a jury of my peers."

"Fine." Mr. Wilks looked around the classroom. "Is there anyone here that will speak out for Madeline? Did anyone see Billy try to cheat off her test?"

The room was silent.

"Just one person," Mr. Wilks said, a small smile quirking at the corner of his lips. He was enjoying this far too much. He and Billy would probably share a big laugh about this on the basketball court after school. "Is there even one person here that will speak out in Miss Starr's defense?"

The other students kept their eyes averted, staring down at their own tests, not willing to risk Billy's wrath by sticking up for me. "Come on," I begged the class, scanning the room for members of the manga club, but seeing no friendly faces. "Someone tell him. You can't let Billy bully you all forever. You have the power to tell the truth."

"*You're* the bully," Lucy scoffed, picking at her pink polished fingernail. "You hurt our friend. And now you want someone to lie for you about it?"

It was then that I noticed Chad, staring down at his hands, gnawing on his lower lip.

"Chad?" I begged, latching on to my one hope. It was a long shot, I knew. Still, he'd promised that day at the restaurant he wouldn't stand by and watch anymore. Was that just lip service? "Please," I begged. "Tell him the truth."

Mr. Wilks turned to Chad. I watched, holding my breath, as Billy's lapdog swallowed hard. He opened his mouth, then closed it again.

"Come on, Chad," Billy said, twisting around in his chair to face his friend. "Tell them you saw her cheat off me."

Chad's face grew red. He opened his mouth again. "I . . ." he began, his voice trembling. "Billy was trying to cheat off Maddy," he blurted out. "He tried to grab her paper. She elbowed him in self-defense."

I let out a sigh of relief.

"What?" Billy's face was red as a tomato. "Chad! What are you doing, man?"

"It's the truth," Chad retorted. "And you know it. Don't be a baby 'cause you got caught."

Mr. Wilks sighed deeply.

"Man, retirement couldn't come too soon," he muttered, running a hand through his thinning gray hair. "Fine," he said, addressing the class. "Everyone go back to your test. But I'll be watching. If I see even one person glance in the direction of someone else's test, you're all going to fail. There will be no passing Go. No collecting anything higher than an F grade."

"But, Coach—" Billy protested.

Mr. Wilks glared at him. "Shut up, Billy. Or I'll send both of you down to Principal Miller's office right now and let him figure this mess out."

Billy clamped his mouth shut.

I glanced back at Chad, relieved and grateful beyond belief. He gave me a small grin. I smiled back, then looked down at my test, not wanting to get in any more trouble or end up making the whole class fail on my account.

I marked down the next answer. Trying to focus and concentrate on the rest of the test while butterflies tripped through my stomach. He stood up for me. Chad Murray, Hater, stood up for me. He saved me from being suspended. Even at the risk of catching total hell from Billy after class.

I knew he was different from the rest of them. I just knew it.

• • •

Later that afternoon, I passed Chad in the hall and was surprised to see him sporting a black eye. A black eye he definitely hadn't had earlier today when he was defending my honor in science class.

"What happened?" I asked, though I had a pretty good idea as to the answer.

"Three guesses," he said with a small laugh. "And the first two don't count."

"Billy," I replied, stating the obvious. "Does it hurt?"

"Nah."

"Look, I'm really sorry," I said, feeling guilty.

"Why? You didn't do it."

"I know. But it's not like it would have happened if you hadn't stood up for me in class."

"I told the truth, as I promised," he said with a sheepish shrug. "Anyone would have done the same."

"Yeah, right. No one would have. No one did, in fact. Except you."

"Look, Billy may have been my best friend for a long time, but let's face it, he's a jerk. A bully," Chad replied. "And someone had to put him in his place. I figured maybe as the best friend it was my job to do it, right?"

"Well, I just wanted to thank you," I said, not sure what else to say. "You're like . . . my knight in shining armor today." I could feel my face burning in a blush. But it was true. And he had really saved me. If I'd gotten a suspension . . .

Chad chuckled. "I don't know about that," he said, and I suddenly realized he was blushing pretty hard himself. "But you are very welcome all the same." He stared down at his feet for a moment, then looked up, catching my eyes in his beautiful blue ones. "By the way?" he added.

"Yeah?"

"If you think my eye's bad, you should see the other guy's."

I started laughing. Chad had punched Billy back? I would have so liked to have seen that. I held out my hand and we slapped high fives. Something I never in a million years would have expected to do with Chad Murray.

"That is the best thing I've heard in . . . well, like, ever," I said. "In fact—"

"Maddy!" a voice down the hall suddenly interrupted. I cringed. Matt. Way to ruin a moment. The guy seriously had a knack.

"I've got to run to class," Chad said apologetically. "I'll see you around?"

"Uh, yeah. Definitely."

"Maddy!" Matt again, more insistent this time. And closer, too. There was no way to avoid him now. I waved a good-bye to Chad and reluctantly turned to face Matt. This was it. I had to come clean. Be honest. Let him know the truth about Sir Leo and Allora so we could move on past this weirdness. It was the only fair, right thing to do.

"Did you see Billy?" he asked in his most giddy voice. "Rumor has it Chad punched him out after chem class." He paused and looked at me pointedly. "After defending you," he added. "So spill. Since when is Chad Murray all hero boy?"

My heart ached for Matt. He was going to be disappointed when he found out. I so didn't want to hurt his feelings. Was there a way I could break it to him gently?

"Matt, we have to talk."

He laughed. "Ooh, sounds ominous. Okay. Talk."

I looked around the crowded hallway. "Not here. Let's find an empty classroom."

We settled on a language lab that wasn't currently being used. I sat down at one of the stations and Matt sat across from me, curiosity clear on his face. Poor guy. He had no idea what I was going to say.

I took a deep breath. This was it. Might as well get it over with.

"Matt, I don't know how to go about this, so I'm just going to say it," I started. I paused, then blurted out, "I'm Allora."

I waited for his reaction. Horror, delight, confusion, maybe a little of each?

Or . . . a blank stare.

"Um, I'm Allora," I repeated, in case he hadn't heard me. "You know, from Fields of Fantasy."

Matt continued to look at me with a confused expression. "Uh, congratulations?"

"Look, I know you're Sir Leo. I figured it out."

"Sir who? What?"

He wasn't making this confession any easier. "Come on, Matt. Fess up. I know you're him. It's okay. You don't have to pretend."

Matt held up his hands. "I have no idea what you're talking about. But I can tell you for a fact, I'm definitely *not* Sir Leo, whoever that is."

I stared at him, confused as all get-out. I couldn't be wrong. There was no way. "B-but . . ." I stammered. "But you have to be him. You're in drama. You like comic books and you play video games. You met someone online."

"Maddy, can you back up a bit? You've completely lost me. What does my being in drama have to do with this Sir Leo guy?"

And so I explained. About my adventures in Fields of Fantasy. My online romance with Sir Leo. How I figured out that Sir Leo had to be Matt. "Which was really confusing," I confessed. " 'Cause I don't feel anything for you. I mean, I love Sir Leo online, but in person . . . well, there's just no spark between us."

Matt stared at me for a moment, then broke out in laughter. "Of course there's no spark, silly," he said. "I'm gay."

I did a double take. "Wh-what?"

"Has it escaped your attention that I like boys? No offense—you're a cool girl. But you're still a girl. It'd never work out," Matt clarified. "Oh, but the person I met online? Eduardo. Beautiful olive-skinned Cuban who lives in Miami. I'm totally smitten." He laughed. "I can't believe you thought I liked you!"

I couldn't believe it. I'd been wrong. Totally and utterly wrong this whole time. Matt wasn't Sir Leo! Not even close. I felt an overwhelming sense of relief.

But the question remained. Who the heck was Sir Leo?

"Then who . . . who could Sir Leo be?" I wondered aloud, racking my brain for a suitable answer. "I mean, he sounds just like you."

Matt shrugged. "Give me what you know and I'll play Veronica Mars."

I counted off the facts on my fingers. "He goes to our school. He's in drama. Likes comic books. He joined the manga club recently. He lives with his dad who works at a bank. . . ."

Matt rolled his eyes. "Oh, that's easy," he said.

"You . . . you know?" I asked, suddenly fearful of finding out.

"Sure. Funny, too, considering today's events."

"Huh?"

"Maddy, you're describing Chad Murray."

My world dropped out from under me. "Chad . . . Chad Murray?" I repeated.

"Sure," Matt said. "Drama, check. Comic books—saw him reading one in study hall—stuffed inside a *Sports Illustrated*, of course. He joined your manga club last week and his dad works with mine at Citizen's Bank."

I felt like I was going to throw up. Sir Leo was Chad Murray? Chad Murray was Sir Leo? I'd been playing Fields of Fantasy this entire time with Chad Murray? Talking, sharing, laughing with Chad Murray? Chad Murray of the Haters? Chad Murray the guy I'd had the biggest crush on since day one of Hannah Dustin High?

Whoa.

WHAT'S WRONG, Maddy?" Ms. Reilly asked.

"Uh, nothing," I lied, dabbing my paintbrush into a pot of shimmery blue. After my conversation with Matt, I'd skipped study hall and retreated to the library to work on my manga. I knew I must look a mess, but I couldn't help it. All I could think of was what Matt had revealed.

Sir Leo was Chad. Chad was Sir Leo. It was like a beautiful dream and a horrific nightmare all rolled into one.

My mind whirled in never-ending circles over the situation and I still had no idea what I was supposed to do about it. Should I tell Chad that I was Allora? What would he say? Would he be happy or totally weirded out? Would he still want to date me in real life like he'd mentioned in the game? Or would he be horrified that his online gamer girl turned out to be real-life Freak Girl? What if he reacted like I had when I'd thought Sir Leo was Matt? I didn't think I could take the disappointment in his beautiful blue eyes when he found out the truth. And I knew I couldn't take the rejection that would follow that disappointment.

Sure, he stood up for me in class. Even got into a fight with his best friend over it all. But just because he felt bad for me did not mean he'd want to date me. He was Chad Murray, after all. He could have anyone in school. Why would he waste his time with little old me?

"Your book is coming out beautifully," my teacher commented, studying my picture. "You must be almost ready to turn it in."

"Yeah," I said. "The judging is on Sunday at the Boston Public Library. So I've got to be done by then."

I rinsed my paintbrush and then chose a vibrant red for Allora's robe. "I'm not painting every scene though," I explained. "Most of it can stay in black and white. I just figured I'd do a cool cover for it."

"Makes sense. Whatever you can do to make your entry stand out is a good thing." Ms. Reilly picked up one of the pages and studied it. It was from the final chapter of the book. The one where Allora goes back into the game to ask Sir Leo if he'll return with her to the real world. Because even though at this point she's vanquished the bullies through her superpowers and made a million new friends and is no longer the Freak Girl outcast at her school, there's still something missing for her. Life isn't complete without her true love by her side.

In the book, of course, Sir Leo is overjoyed to return to Earth with his gamer girl. The jury was still out on my own happy ending. And that made it nearly impossible for me to get up the energy to finish the final panel. The one where Sir Leo is supposed to sweep Allora into his arms and kiss her sweetly, declaring his undying love for his all-powerful, beautiful gamer girl. It was one of the most important drawings in the entire book, and yet I couldn't bring myself to work on it. I just kept thinking that my real-life love story might not end that way.

"I think you have a good chance, Maddy," Ms. Reilly observed. "I really do. I know as a teacher I'm supposed to say encouraging things like that, but in this case it's the truth. Your drawings are just as good, if not better, than what I've seen in bookstores. And your story line is a lot of fun, too."

"Thanks." A lump formed in my throat and I struggled to swallow it down. She was so nice. And she'd done so much for me. Why couldn't I be more appreciative? Why did my brain keep wandering back to Sir Leo/Chad territory?

She set down the page and looked at me pointedly. "So now do you mind telling me what's wrong?" she asked, her voice leaving little room for argument.

I set down the paintbrush and scrubbed my face with my hands. Maybe I *should* just tell her. It was too hard to keep it all inside, eating away at me. And if anyone would understand, it was probably Ms. Reilly.

"Allora and Sir Leo . . ." I began, pointing at the characters on the page. "They're . . . well, they're based on my playing Fields of Fantasy."

Ms. Reilly nodded. "I figured maybe," she said with a small smile.

"My dad gave me the game about a month ago for my birthday. So I could play with him because my parents are divorced now."

"Right. I remember your telling me that."

"Yeah. Except he's never online." I frowned. "Or he's too busy with his other friends to play with me. So I started playing with this other kid. Sir Leo." I pointed to his character. "And we started to get to know each other really well."

"Right. This guy, he's not . . . pressuring you to meet him, is he?" Ms. Reilly said, going all worried adult on me for a moment.

"Well, yeah, but it's not like you're thinking. He's not some lonely old man."

"How do you know?"

"Because he goes here. I figured out who he is."

Relief washed over her face. "Okay, that's good. I was worried for a moment you were going to say you had some kind of weird online predator." She cocked her head. "So why are you upset?"

"'Cause he's one of the Haters."

"The Haters?" The corner of Ms. Reilly's lip curled into a smile. "Who are the Haters?"

"You know, Billy and his crew. They're popular, but total bullies."

Ms. Reilly nodded. "Ah, those guys. So your Sir Leo is one of them?"

I hung my head. "Yes. It stinks. I like him so much and in the game he likes me back and he wants to meet me, but if he found out who I am . . ."

"You think he'd go running in the other direction."

"Right."

I waited for Ms. Reilly to give typical adult advice about my being a beautiful girl, one any guy would be lucky to have, but she didn't. Instead, she sat looking thoughtful for a moment, then nodded her head.

"I can see your dilemma," she said. "You want to keep playing, but you're afraid if he finds out the truth, your virtual romance will end."

"Yeah." I nodded. "You probably think I'm being stupid, huh?"

"Not at all. But at the same time, you can't just go on like this. You'll drive yourself crazy."

"I think I already have."

"You really don't have any choice but to tell him," Ms. Reilly said. "Let him know who you are. You never know. He may surprise you."

"Yeah, right."

"Well, you obviously see something in him that's special, right? Something that's made you fall for him? So how about you give him a little credit? Give him a chance to make good. And if he turns you down, well, then at least you know. And you can move on. And if he doesn't . . . well, this could be the start of something really great, no?"

"Yeah, but . . ."

"But you're afraid of losing him. I get it. It's scary to imagine the guy you love running in the other direction. And I'm not saying it might not happen. But think about it. What do you have to lose? Nothing but a fantasy world you've conjured up in a virtual reality game and in your head."

"Yeah, I guess." I stared down at the cover. Allora shooting fire from her fingers, vanquishing the bullies with a self-satisfied smirk. If only I could channel some of her confidence . . . "I just want him to like me, you know? And it seems impossible that he would."

"Maddy, listen to me," Ms. Reilly said firmly. "I know it's hard to believe, but not all the kids who run with the popular crowd are the same. Some are really good people who just get mixed up in a scene and aren't strong enough to break away or stand up for themselves. As long as it's not Billy Henderson himself . . ."—she laughed—"then I think you may have a chance."

I nodded slowly. What she said was true. After all, there were all those nights when Sir Leo and I had chatted about the problems he had standing up for himself in front of his friends. And he had done it. Sold out his friend. Stuck up for a girl he thought he barely knew. Taking my advice, without knowing it'd come from me.

Maybe he *would* surprise me. Maybe he'd even be really psyched that it was me.

I firmed my resolve. Ms. Reilly was right. No matter what

the ultimate answer turned out to be, I had to know for sure either way. When I got home from school today, I'd log on and tell Sir Leo the truth. Tell him who I really was and see what happened next.

Like my Gamer Girl, I had to risk it all for love.

21

THAT NIGHT after school, I ran up to my room and switched on my computer. My heart was racing in nervous anticipation and my fingers shook, making it difficult to type. But I could do this. I was strong. I could handle whatever happened.

Maybe.

Maybe not.

Ugh.

The loading screen appeared and I typed in my user name and password. A moment later Allora appeared on the screen, right where I left her. She smiled up at me encouragingly. Of course *she* had no worries. She only knew sweet, knightly Sir Leo who brought her flowers and held her hand while gazing lovingly into her perfect blue eyes.

"Ready for the moment of truth, Allora?" I whispered to her.

I typed in the command to make her nod. That was the

good thing about video game characters. They always agreed with you.

"Okay, then. Here goes nothing."

[Allora] Greetings, Sir Leo.

No response at first and I worried that my not being online much the past week, thinking I was avoiding talking to Matt, was making him standoffish.

[SirLeo] adssfagafds
[Allora] ???
[SirLeo] Sorry. Bad typing. Whats up?
[Allora] (I wanted to talk to you about something. Can we meet somewhere?)
[SirLeo] Uh, shore.
[Allora] (Hm, looks like you're in the Elf Tree Inn, huh? Stay put. I'll be there in a second.)
[SirLeo] ok.

I maneuvered Allora through the busy town streets and walked her into the elfin inn Sir Leo and I had spent so much time hanging out in. It took me a second to locate my knight, as he wasn't in his normal chair. Instead, he was at the bar, downing beers. Must have been one of those days for him, too.

[Allora] I'm here.

Allora waves.
Sir Leo whistles.
[SirLeo] Helllllo hottie!
[Allora] (LOL.)

I could feel my face blushing, then scolded myself for being self-conscious about the compliments my video game character received. What he thought of the real-life me would be much more important. I glanced in the mirror beside my computer, tucking a strand of black hair behind my ear. If only I'd created a character that looked even remotely like the real-life me. Then maybe it wouldn't be such a shock to him.

I shook my head and turned back to the game.

[Allora] (So before we go questing, I wanted to talk.)
[SirLeo] ok.
[Allora] (It's been sooo fun playing with you. And I'm sorry I've seemed weirded out every time you ask me personal stuff. It's not that I don't want to tell you things. I've felt weird about the irl versus online thing.)

No response from Sir Leo. I took a deep breath and kept typing.

[Allora] (So I've changed my mind. I would like to meet up with you.)
[SirLeo] Kewl. On a date with a hot elf chick. Rock on.
[Allora] (LOL! I'm trying to be serious here!)

[SirLeo] OK. So when do you want to get together?

[Allora] (Wait, before we figure that out, I want you to know that I've figured out who you are. We go to the same school, actually.)

[SirLeo] LOL. Who am I then???

[Allora] (Chad Murray.)

[SirLeo] LOL yes. You are right! So who are you?

My fingers froze. My breath caught in my throat. For a moment I couldn't type. But I was at the point of no return. Here went nothing.

[Allora] (I'm Maddy Starr.)

[Sir Leo] OMG u're Freak Girl!!!!!

Sir Leo laughs.

[SirLeo] LOL LOL LOL. No way!

I stared at the screen, my every nightmare coming true. Here I'd been hoping, praying, it'd all be okay. Obviously I'd just been kidding myself. My heart plummeted to my stomach as all my fantasies were flushed down the toilet in one fell swoop.

I was a joke to him. A freaking joke. I wanted to die.

[SirLeo] Dude, and here I thought you were some totally hot chick. Not the goth-y-looking witch that goes to our school. That's just too hilarious.

[Allora] Why is that funny? And I'm not a witch. Or a goth.

[SirLeo] Whatever, dude. I can't believe you actually thought you'd have a chance with someone like Chad Murray. LOL LOL LOL.

Tears blurred my vision and I could barely read what he wrote. But I could see enough. More than enough to break my heart.

[Allora] Well, I guess I know how you feel now. And so this is good-bye.
Sir Leo laughs.
[SirLeo] Sayonara, Freak Girl.

I reached down and switched off my computer, not even bothering to shut it down correctly. I didn't care if it crashed. In fact, at this moment I didn't care if the whole world crashed, careening off its axis and spiraling straight toward the apocalypse.

It was over. Over forever. I'd dared. I'd risked. I'd gambled it all.

And I'd lost.

It was over. The crazy dream had morphed into a terrible nightmare. The hope I'd had of going out, bridging a gap, showing the world that cliques don't make a bit of difference when two people were really, truly in love? Crushed. Smashed. Shattered. Like Grandma's babies. Gone forever.

My heart ached in my chest as my brain tried to mass-dump all its fantasies of what could have happened. All those crazy daydreams I'd stored up of Chad and me. Holding hands in the school hallways. Kissing by the lockers. Cuddling on the bleachers. Going out on a real date. Making out at the movies.

I squeezed my eyes shut and pinched myself, praying this was all some crazy bizarre dream that I'd soon wake up from. But it was no use. This was reality. My reality.

I hated him. Hated, hated, hated him. I wanted to run to his house and punch him in the stomach. Tear at his face with my fingernails until he bled. Something—anything—to make him feel as horrible as I felt right now.

But I couldn't. I had to retain some pride. I would go to school the next day and face the Haters like I didn't have a care in the world. And when they laughed at me, I would just walk away, head held high.

And pray I won the manga contest so I could have enough cash to pay for next year's tuition at Boston Academy.

I TOSSED and turned all night, alternating crying with vibrant, violent fantasies about how to make Chad's life as miserable as possible. I wanted to hit him, to hurt him, to make him feel as much pain as I felt as I lay there, alone and unwanted. Freak Girl once again.

At the same time I wished I could just go back. Like in that movie *The Matrix* when the guy takes the blue pill. The one that would let him live out his life in ignorance, forgetting the harsh truth of reality. After all, if I didn't know Sir Leo was Chad or if I had never told Chad that I was me, maybe we could have at least continued our sweet, innocent video game romance.

But even as I wished it, I knew it was a stupid thing to want. After all, why would I want to spend my time with someone who thought I was a loser? A freak? Someone less than worthy of his attentions?

Though of course a part of me still did. A very pathetic stupid part.

I squeezed my hands into fists, digging my nails into my palms until I drew blood. I tried to tell myself that at the end of the day, his opinion didn't matter. I wasn't a freak. I wasn't a loser. I had plenty of new friends who thought I was talented and interesting and fun and they chose to spend time with me. The real me—not some stupid virtual reality version. If Chad Murray wasn't interested in Maddy Starr as a living, breathing person—someone with strengths and weaknesses, talents and flaws—that was his choice. And it didn't reflect at all on the person that I was. Life without Sir Leo, without Fields of Fantasy, would go on. I'd be fine. In fact, I'd be more than fine. I didn't need him.

So I dressed, choosing a bright-colored baby doll dress that said I didn't have a care in the world. I grabbed my books and my keys, then looked around for my sketchbook. It wasn't in my room. I must have left it at school. Thinking back, I remembered working on it in the library before Ms. Reilly came by, but couldn't remember if I'd grabbed it on the way out. A small worry tugged at my brain. What if I'd left it in the library? No one would have walked off with it, would they? My contest entry was in there. All my original drawings.

I tried to rationalize away the bubbling panic in my throat. How could I have been so stupid? What if someone had found them? What if . . . ? No. I couldn't even think of that!

I had to get to school, now!

. . .

Black Raven approached me as I jumped off the bus at school, her already normally white powdered face looking more than a bit pasty.

I squinted my eyes at her. "What's wrong?" I asked, a feeling of dread washing over me. For some reason I just knew this had to be about my drawings.

She didn't say anything at first, just looked at me with a pained expression.

"You're scaring me," I said, shoving my trembling hands in my pockets.

"Uh, I think you'd better sit down," she replied, grabbing me by the wrist and dragging me over to a bench. She sat down next to me, taking both my hands in her own. Her black fingernail polish was half chipped off, as if she'd picked at each nail. "Did you leave copies of your contest entry at school yesterday?" she asked.

I suddenly felt like I was going to throw up. "Um, I think I might have left my sketchbook in the library at lunch," I told her.

"But those were copies, right? Not your originals? Or you have copies somewhere? At home, maybe?"

"Um, no. Those were my originals," I said. "I was going to copy them when I was done this weekend. Get Kinko's to bind them into a book." I caught her eyes in mine, my heart beating a mile a minute. "What's going on, Blackie?"

She dropped my gaze, staring down at her lap, swearing under her breath.

"Blackie?"

"Those jerks," she whispered. "I'm going to beat their faces in."

"What happened?"

"Maddy, someone stole your drawings. And they . . . well, they added stuff to them."

I stared at her, heart wrenching inside my chest. This wasn't happening. It was a dream. Or something. My drawings. They couldn't be . . .

"Added stuff . . . ?" I croaked, unable to summon up much more than that.

"You know, like . . . mustaches. Devil horns. And they . . . well, they hung them all around school."

I was going to pass out. Right then, right there. Keel over and let the blackness take me. If I was lucky maybe I'd hit my head and go into a coma or something. Anything so I wouldn't have to deal with this nightmare reality.

"Billy . . ." I mouthed. It had to be him. Unless it was Chad. I knew he didn't want to be with me. I knew he thought I was Freak Girl. But could he really . . . ?

"Actually, word on the street—or in the halls, I guess—was that it was Chelsea and Lucy," Black Raven informed me. "Amy was in the bathroom and she heard the twins, Grace and Gemma, giggling about it. But I'm sure it was on Billy's orders. Those two won't blow their own noses without him giving permission first."

I slowly rose from the bench, my legs wobbling, trying

to regain my composure. Tears slipped from my eyes and splashed down my cheeks. I wanted to brush them away, but my hands didn't seem to want to work right.

I couldn't believe it. My book, with my very personal story line, was not only ruined, but currently hanging around school for everyone and anyone to look at. What would people say when they saw Allora blasting the Billy look-alike with fire from her fingers? What would they think when they read how through her adventures she ends up the most popular girl in school? And that wasn't even the worst part. I realized Chad was going to see those drawings, if he hadn't already, and recognize himself as Sir Leo. And he'd know about my stupid crush on him—my pathetic fantasy of making him my real-life boyfriend. It was beyond humiliating.

Black Raven looked up at me, sympathy in her eyes. "I'm so sorry, Maddy," she said. "Whatever you want me to do. You just let me know. I'm here for you."

I nodded numbly and turned to walk into school. Everything seemed to be moving in slow motion as I tried to process what I'd just learned. My contest entry—destroyed. The book I put my heart and soul into—now marked up and ridiculed and put on display for all the school to see. As I walked through the front doors, I could immediately feel the stares, hear the giggles. They were all making fun of me. No surprise there.

I was once again nothing more than a joke.

My eyes fell on a small crowd gathered around a locker.

They were laughing and pointing. I pushed through them to find my drawing. The one of Sir Leo and me cuddled up together, watching the waterfall. Someone had drawn a beard and mustache on Sir Leo and changed the caption from "I love you" to "Wow! I'm stuck with Freak Girl."

I tore the drawing from the wall and pushed my way back out of the crowd, trying to block out the laughter and jeers. Not ten feet down the hall there was another scene, similarly doctored up. And another was posted a few feet from that one.

All my hard work, all the hours I'd spent perfecting each panel. And in one evening, two girls who hated me because I didn't live up to their standards of cool had seen fit to destroy it all, ruining my chance to win the contest and humiliating me in front of the whole school.

I dropped the two drawings I'd recovered on the ground. I didn't even want to touch them anymore.

The dream was over. The Haters had won. There would be no happy ending for me.

Then, just when I thought my morning couldn't get any worse, I saw Chad and Billy down the end of the hall, in the middle of what appeared a heated conversation. They must have made up from the fight they'd had. Not surprising, I guessed.

Chad looked up and saw me.

I turned and fled.

I know, I know, not very brave of me. I should have

stalked over to him and punched him in the face. Or spit on him, at the very least. But I couldn't help it. I no longer felt strong. And I was too embarrassed to face him now that he'd seen all the romantic drawings I'd sketched of him. So instead I ran down the hallway like a coward, out the front doors, past the buses, and across the parking lot. I stopped when I got to the edge of the school grounds. I gave one last look at the school, then started walking down the street toward home.

I arrived at Grandma's house about an hour later, sweaty and exhausted from the walk.

I noticed Mom's car in the driveway. Great. She was home from work. Just what I needed to make my day complete. She was going to kill me for leaving school.

Whatever. I didn't even care. I pulled open the screen door and trudged inside.

"I'm, uh, not feeling well," I shouted, in the direction of the kitchen. "So I, uh, came home from school. I'll be in my room."

Mom was in front of me a split second later, her hand on my forehead. How she cleared the living room that fast was beyond me. Some weird mom powers, I guess.

"What's wrong? Is it your head? Your stomach? Do you have cramps? Are you feverish?"

No, Mom, my heart is broken, I'm the laughingstock of school, and everything I've worked for has been destroyed. And the guy I love thinks I'm a loser freak.

"I just don't feel good," I said. "I'm going to take a nap."

"Maddy, you look like you're going to cry," Mom said, studying me with concerned eyes.

"I'm fine," I managed to choke out past the huge lump in my throat.

There was no way Mom was buying that.

"Go up to your room," she instructed. "I'll make some tomato soup and grilled cheese and be up in a few."

I smiled a little. Tomato soup and grilled cheese sandwiches was my favorite meal ever. When I was younger I use to fake sick just so Mom would make it. "Okay," I agreed. "Thanks."

I padded up the stairs and into my room. My computer sat in the corner, mocking me. I collapsed on my bed without even bothering to take off my shoes, pulling myself into a ball and hugging my knees to my chest.

Just when I thought things were finally getting better, life had imploded on me once again. I couldn't win. I just couldn't win.

Now there would be no contest entry. I'd be stuck at Hannah Dustin until graduation. Stuck dealing with the Haters for another two years.

Could life be any worse?

My mom pushed open my bedroom door a few minutes later, armed with a tray of piping hot soup and perfectly toasted sandwiches. I sat up and she set the tray over my lap, then took a seat on the edge of the bed. I picked up my spoon and dunked it in the soup, bringing the steaming liquid to my mouth.

"Mmm, mmm, good?" she quipped.

"Definitely," I said, setting down the spoon and grabbing half the grilled cheese. Mom had cut off the crusts, just as I used to like it as a kid. Guilt washed over me as I thought about how ungrateful I'd been over the last months.

"I'm sorry I'm such a lousy daughter," I said, taking a bite of sandwich.

Mom surprised me with a laugh. "What makes you think you're a lousy daughter?"

I rolled my eyes. "Come on. I've been nothing but a jerk since we sold the house and moved here and everyone knows it."

"Okay, fine," Mom admitted with a small smile. "You haven't been the most pleasant person to be around, it's true. But you need to give yourself a break, too, you know. You've been through a lot this year."

"You don't know the half of it," I muttered, mouth full of cheese.

"Probably not. But I'm your mother. And I think I know you a little better than perhaps you give me credit for." She reached over and brushed a wayward strand of hair from my face. "Obviously moving has been rough on you. And I feel so bad for making you switch schools in the middle of the year, leaving all your friends behind." She sighed. "At the time, I didn't see any other solution. I was so angry at your father. . . ."

"Why? What did he do? You never told us." Maybe this time I'd finally get to hear the truth. "Why did you leave him?"

Mom considered the question for a moment. "Your father is a wonderful man in many ways," she said. "He's very fun. Outgoing. Enthusiastic about whatever he throws himself into. When we were first together, we had a blast. He was always making me laugh." She stared off into the distance, remembering. "But after having two kids, I wanted a stable life for you two. It couldn't be all fun and games anymore. In a sense, I finally grew up." She picked up a photo of Dad from my nightstand and studied it. "But your father never did."

I nodded, thinking back to all the times recently that Dad had acted more childish than my eight-year-old sister.

"He let me down over and over again with his irresponsible choices. It was like having a third kid instead of a partner." Mom set down the photo. "Frankly, I grew tired of it."

"Yeah," I said, staring down at the ground. As much as I wished to ignore it, I could see her point. Why would she want to be married to someone like that?

"It was hard to make the decision I did. Mainly because I knew it would affect the two of you so much. It tore me apart to pull you out of school and see you suffer here. But I didn't feel I had much of a choice. I couldn't live life as I had been. I just couldn't."

My heart went out to my mother. She'd been so strong to make a change in her life to get what she needed. And what had I done in return? Acted like a brat. Selfishly whining about my own situation, not even thinking about how hard it had been for her.

"The good news is," my mother continued, "that I'm happier now." She stroked my hair. "I want to be a good mother to you guys."

"You are, Mom," I said. And I meant it. "I'm proud of you."

"I don't want you to blame your father either," she added sternly. "That's part of the reason I haven't really talked about this to you guys. He's a good man in many ways and he tries really hard. He and I are just two different people and our lives are taking two separate paths. But that has nothing to do with his loving you and Emily. He adores the two of you. Even if he can be a schmuck at times."

I laughed at the last bit. "I know. I don't . . . blame him. I just . . . well, I wish things were different, you know?"

"Right. Well, I certainly can understand that. It's not how I wanted things either. But unfortunately life doesn't always deal out happily-ever-afters—at least not in the way you're expecting."

I thought about Chad. The contest. "Right," I said.

"But you have to take control of your destiny. And sometimes that's not easy." She reached up and brushed a strand of hair from my eyes. "Okay, I spilled my guts," she said with a small smile. "Your turn."

"All right, fine. I was going to enter this contest," I explained, trying not to get all choked up again. "Design a manga and maybe get it published. The prize money would have been enough to cover tuition at Boston Academy." I sighed. "But now I'm left with nothing."

I explained what had happened with my drawings. About Billy and Chad, Lucy and Chelsea. Everything except the online romance I'd shared with Sir Leo/Chad. That was still too painful to admit aloud and Mom would probably just give me some lecture about playing too many video games, just like my father.

"Oh, honey, I'm so sorry," Mom said, sympathy clouding her eyes. "Do you want me to call the principal? Those kids should be punished. They shouldn't get away with something like that."

"No, thank you." I shook my head. "That'll just make them hate me more."

"I know, but . . ." Mom started. "Maybe you can at least go to the judges on Sunday and see if they'll give you an extension or something."

"Yeah, right," I said, looking glumly at the flyer.

"Seriously, Maddy. Think about it. I mean, it can't hurt, right? I mean, if you explained what happened, maybe they'd at least give you some feedback, even if you couldn't win the actual contest."

"Maybe . . . I don't know." The last thing I wanted to do was explain to my manga hero Svetlana what a loser I was.

"Well, it's your choice. But remember what I said about taking control of your destiny." Mom rose from the bed and headed out of the room. She stopped at the door. "If you can learn that now, it'll save you a lot of pain and trouble down the road."

"Thanks, Mom," I said, tossing her a half smile. "I love you."

"I love you, too. And Maddy?"

"Yeah?"

"I'm proud of you."

And all of a sudden I knew exactly what I had to do.

So THAT'S what led me to be sitting on a splintery wooden bench in the Boston Public Library Sunday night, along with dozens of other kids, waiting for their turn to face the judges. Some chatted in low whispers, others giggled to one another in nervous anticipation. Still others stared at the ground, eyes wide, faces pale, fingers trembling as they pressed their portfolios close to their chests.

I wouldn't have been frightened if I'd had my manga still. I believed in my story and art and would have faced the judges with confidence, knowing that *Gamer Girl* was sure to impress them. If nothing else, I'd learned to believe in myself and my abilities.

But tonight all the self-confidence in the world wasn't going to cut it. I had no contest entry. Just a few scrap drawings I'd managed to salvage after the attack. The judges would probably laugh in my face and send me on my way empty-handed and defeated.

But I had to take that risk. I had to try. As Mom had said,

I needed to take control of my own destiny. And as Ms. Reilly had said, I couldn't let *them* win.

Besides, I reminded myself, I would at the very least get to see some of my heroes tonight. Svetlana was judging and I was dying to meet her and tell her how much I loved *Drama-con*. Maybe get her to sign my copy of her book. That would make the trip to Boston worth it, in and of itself.

Suddenly, without warning, the door burst open and the biting wind whooshed through the hall, scattering papers and sending kids scrambling for their artwork. I looked over, wondering who had arrived so late and caused such a disturbance. My eyes fell on a lone figure, silhouetted in the doorway, intently scanning the room.

It was a figure I'd know anywhere.

My heart raced and my stomach twisted in Boy Scout-strength knots as I tried to shield myself behind the person next to me.

Why was he here? Hadn't he done enough already?

But the girl I ducked behind was too short to hide me. And a moment later I heard him call out my name.

"Maddy, I have to talk to you," he said.

But I wasn't interested in talking. Not to him. Not after his betrayal. Jumping up from the bench, I ran down the hall, ignoring the protests from the others that I was cutting in line. I reached the end of the hall and turned left, then right, then left again. My only thought—to get away from him.

"Maddy!" I heard him call. "Wait up!"

I took another turn and found myself at a dead end. I was

trapped with no way to escape. His footsteps echoed on the stone floor as he approached. He was breathing hard from the chase.

"Maddy . . ." He paused, then, in a softer voice. "Allora . . ."

Drawing in a deep breath, I forced myself to turn around slowly. To face him with bravery I didn't feel.

"Well, well, Sir Leo," I greeted in my coldest voice. "We meet at last."

Chad Murray blushed deep red, then, to my surprise, got down on one knee and bowed before me. "M'lady," he greeted, faking an English accent as I'd heard him do onstage. "I have searched for thee, far and wide. I am so lucky to have found you."

It seemed cornier in real life, somehow. But at the same time, kind of sweet. My heart ached as I looked down at him. Why was he doing this? Making it harder. It wasn't fair.

I forced myself to remain cold and aloof. I didn't want him to see me cry. "How dare you come here," I rebuked him, folding my arms across my chest. "Haven't you done enough?"

"No. I need you to listen to me."

"You've said enough online."

He scrambled to his feet. "I said nothing online."

"Yeah, right." I snorted. "Selective memory loss? Well, let me remind you, then. You called me a witch, a goth. A freak. All the things Billy is always saying."

He nodded eagerly. "Exactly. All the things Billy says.

Maddy, think about it. Have I *ever* called you one of those names?"

"Um, well, not to my face," I admitted. "But that doesn't mean—"

"Look, Maddy," he continued, in a rushed voice. "Billy came over my house on Thursday night. He said he wanted to apologize and stuff. So I invited him in and we went up to my room to talk. I left him alone for a few minutes when my dad needed me to take out the trash. I forgot I'd been logged into Fields of Fantasy. Billy found the game and started messing with my character, thinking he was being funny. You IMed *him*, not me." He caught my eyes with his own pleading ones. "Do you see where I'm going with this?"

"But . . . but . . ." I stammered. Could he be telling the truth? Could it really have been Billy saying those horrible things to me? Could I have been wishing death and dismemberment on the wrong Hater? It seemed impossible, yet in another way it made perfect sense.

Chad reached over and grabbed my hands in his, squeezing them in a way that made my butterflies flutter through my stomach, against my better judgment. "You've got to believe me," he said, looking upset and tortured. "I didn't know. After Billy left Thursday night, I went online looking for you. But you weren't there. And the next day at school I saw those pictures . . . your manga. Those scenes of Sir Leo and Allora—and realized the truth. I was such an idiot not to have figured it out sooner." He shook his head.

"Well, I tried not to give a lot away," I grudgingly gave him.

"Then I heard Lucy and Chelsea and Billy laughing about what they'd done. Ugh! I was so mad. I mean, how could they do that? Destroy something you worked so hard on without even a second thought. I totally went off on them. Someone had to, and I've stood around way too long letting them get away with this stuff. I realized it was time to take a stand for once in my life."

I raised an eyebrow. "Really? You told them off?"

"Yes," Chad said with a nod. "And then I reported them to the principal. The three of them got suspended." He sighed. "If only I'd done something earlier, instead of standing back like a coward. Then you'd still have your drawings." He squeezed his hands into fists. "I'm so sorry, Maddy."

I hesitated. I did want to forgive him. I did. In fact, at that very moment I wanted nothing more than to throw myself into his arms and hug him to death. But at the same time, I was scared. What if this was all some sort of setup? A trick? I couldn't bear to let myself buy his story and end up being burned all over again.

"Why should I believe you?" I asked, trying to keep my voice even.

"Because of this." Chad reached into his messenger bag and pulled out a bound book. My eyes widened as I saw the cover. *Gamer Girl*. It was my manga. The cover page I'd painted still intact.

"What the . . . ?" I questioned, taking the book in my

hands. I opened it with shaking fingers. "How did you . . . ?"

I gasped at what I saw inside. My story. My words. Just as I'd written them. But while some of the sketches were mine, others had been altered. Drawn by different hands. Each page illustrated in its own style, all coming together to tell the story of Allora and Sir Leo that I'd created.

It was the most beautiful thing I'd ever seen in all my life.

I looked up at Chad, overwhelmed. "I don't understand," I said, no longer caring that my voice was choked and confused.

He smiled, looking proud. "I blackmailed Lucy into giving me back the rest of the drawings—the ones she hadn't messed with. Then I went around school and collected the others. I had Ms. Reilly call an emergency meeting of the manga club and I explained what happened to everyone. We divided up the pages between us and everyone went home and worked all weekend to re-create your book. Then today I brought it to Kinko's and had it copied and bound." He paused, then added, "I checked the entry rules. It's perfectly okay to have more than one artist contribute to the book. And at the end of the day, *Gamer Girl* is still your story. You can enter it and win the publication you deserve."

"You guys fixed my book?" I cried, tears streaming down my cheeks. "You did this for me?"

"Of course, silly," Chad replied, reaching over to touch me on the shoulder. "You're not alone, you know. You have many, many people who care about you." He gestured behind him. "They're all waiting for you outside. Blackie, Sarah, Ed,

David, Jessie, Amy, Matt. The whole club took a bus to Boston to cheer you on. You're the only one here with your own fan club." He grinned.

My heart caught in my throat. I stared down at the manga entry. "It's beautiful," I whispered. "Better than I could have even imagined it." I looked up at Chad. At Sir Leo. My virtual knight in shining armor come to life in the most amazing way possible. "Thank you," I murmured, though the words seemed so inadequate, given the circumstances. "I don't know how to even—"

He pressed a hand to my mouth, shushing me. "My lady dost protest too much," he murmured, lapsing back into Sir Leo speech. Then he reached out and took my hand in his own, stroking the back of my palm with soft fingers. A chill tripped down my spine at his touch. Reality was even more delicious than I'd imagined it would be.

I smiled at him, finally letting go of the hate and suspicion I'd held on to for so long. For the first time in a long time I felt I could trust someone. Completely.

Even if I didn't place in the contest, I'd won. I'd won in more ways than I could even count. And the Haters had lost. From now on, they could do their worst—it didn't matter. They had no power over me. Just like my heroine, I was a real gamer girl now. And that made me a winner.

I had friends. I had family. I had Chad Murray, aka Sir Leo.

"Are you disappointed Allora turned out to be me?" I asked hesitantly, having to get that one last thing out on the table.

"Are you kidding?" Chad asked incredulously, disbelief clear on his beautiful face. "I always thought you were so cool. Well, except maybe that first day in the unicorn sweatshirt." His eyes danced merrily, letting me know he was just teasing.

"I've always kind of had a crush on you, too," I admitted. "I was so torn between liking Sir Leo and liking you. It's crazy that you turned out to be the same guy. Or maybe not so crazy."

He smiled at me then. A beautiful, genuine, amazing smile that made my heart feel like it was going to burst. Chad Murray liked me. The real me. The real-life me.

"When I found out Sir Leo was you, I got scared," I confessed. "I thought someone like you would never give someone like me a second glance."

"Well, you deserve a second glance," he told me in an earnest voice. "And a third and a fourth and a fifth, sixth, and seventh. . . ." He paused, then added, "And Maddy?"

"Yes, Chad?"

"I hope you don't think this is unchivalrous of me. But I think I might die if I don't kiss you now. A real-life kiss."

The butterflies leaped to my throat, choking me. "Well," I said, struggling to get the words out. "Wouldn't want that to happen." I grinned. "After all, then who would tank the dragons in Fields of Fantasy?"

"Good point." He leaned forward and pressed his lips against mine—fantasy becoming reality in a single touch. "A very good point."

AFTER THE judging, everyone headed to Longhorn's for a party. Our group alone filled five tables and the waitstaff was bustling about, trying to fill all our requests. I looked around the restaurant in awe. It was hard to believe everyone was there because of me. To think only a month ago I felt totally friendless and alone.

Mom, Dad, Grandma, and Emily were at one table. Emily was currently demonstrating to Grandma how to stick a spoon on her nose and Mom and Dad were actually talking to each other—even laughing at times. I knew they'd never get back together as husband and wife, but it was nice to see them being civil to each other again. After all, they were both my family and I wanted nothing more than for everyone to get along.

At the next table were my Boston friends. They'd all come out to cheer me on. Caitlin, Ashley, Dana—even David Silverman, who I found out, to my delight, had asked Caitlin out a few days earlier. The two of them were currently snuggled in a booth, looking lovey-dovey at each other. At first Caitlin had been worried about telling me, knowing I once had a crush on him, too, but those days were long over. I had Chad now. Chad, who was currently sitting next to me, holding my hand and looking at me with beautiful, loving blue eyes and making me go all melty inside.

The other tables were packed with manga club members and Ms. Reilly. Blackie, Matt, Sarah, Luke, Jessie, David, Ed, and a ton of other people I didn't even really know but who all seemed to know me. They were all chattering excitedly about the judging and what would happen next.

Yes, *Gamer Girl* was the official winner of the evening. The judges loved the collaborative spirit of the work—praising the way everyone's personal styles melded together into something truly special. And they loved my story line, too, claiming it was the perfect mix of shojo and fantasy. My hero Svetlana gave me the highest praise and told me I definitely had a future in the business. She even took me aside afterward to give me her personal e-mail, saying I should feel free to ask her advice anytime I needed it. Totally made my already unforgettable night.

The manga would now move on to the national competition, where the publisher would choose one regional winner to publish. But while publishing would be a dream come true, sitting here in this restaurant, surrounded by my friends, family, and new boyfriend, I already felt like I won the jackpot.

No longer Freak Girl. Not even Gamer Girl. Just Maddy Starr. And right now, that was enough.